ROGUE'S SON

DARCY FLYNN

Lyn!
Hope you enjoy
Sam & Kit's story!
Best!
Darcy
Flynn

SOUL MATE PUBLISHING

New York

ROGUE'S SON

Copyright©2014

DARCY FLYNN

Cover Design by Rae Monet, Inc.

Published in the United States of America by
Soul Mate Publishing
P.O. Box 24
Macedon, New York, 14502

ISBN: 978-1-61935-431-9
eBook ISBN: 978-1-61935-362-6

www.SoulMatePublishing.com

The publisher does not have any control over and does not assume any responsibility for author or third-party websites or their content.

For Tom, my wrangler husband.

And for Dolly, his champion quarter horse reiner.

Watching you work together in the ring

is one of the most visual pleasures in my life.

Acknowledgements

I want to thank my beta readers, Janet King and Amy Mauldin. The feedback from both of you was priceless. Thanks for being part of my team. And thank you to my incredible, hard-working critique partners, Cindy Brannam and Sharon Hermes. Thanks for your thoughtful critique and for catching those pesky last-minute errors. Thank you to my editor, Debby Gilbert. Your excellent critique made my book even better. Thank you also to Colleen Shanahan, Esq. Thanks for your patience in answering all of my questions. I had no idea how to file a quitclaim and neither did my hero.

And thank you to the two most important men in my life, Tom and Roman. Thank you, Tom, not only for your continued support but for teaching me how to clean tack all those years ago. My heroine also thanks you. And Roman, the inspiration for Macy's boyfriend, thank you for your encouragement and creative input in my life. I love you both.

Chapter 1

This road was exactly as Sam Dawson remembered it. Nothing but gravel and potholes. Not the best terrain for an Audi R8. He had to creep along with caution or his beauty would be chipped to pieces. You'd think after six years the county would have at least had the funds to pave the thing. But times were hard for so many small towns and Sugar Creek was no exception.

Still, it was great to be back home. Even with all of its drought and wildfires, West Texas was in his DNA. It always would be.

As his car crawled around the next bend, Sam rubbed his hand across his well-developed beard. He needed both a shave and a haircut before he presented himself to his employees or they'd be thinking he was some sort of mountain man.

He hadn't planned to come back so soon, and hated that he'd had to cut the Montana wilderness tour short, but when he found out the deal for the Kendall property was off, he decided it was time to step in. Kit didn't know it, but he'd been playing poker with her for quite some time. And he was ready to lay his cards on the table. Well, maybe not all of his cards. But before he did, he needed to be certain she wouldn't dare call his bluff. Her future, the success of McCabe's Lodge, and the economic recovery of Sugar Creek depended on it.

It was all Kit could do not to slam down the phone. Another cancellation, the third this month, and right in the middle of fly-fishing season. She sighed and pushed herself away from the bill-laden desk and stared out the window.

The sight of the clay tennis courts in what used to be her pasture still looked out of place against the rugged West Texas terrain. They were too close to the house and if she had known what the resort had planned to do with her land, she never would have sold it to them. But, when the bill collectors started calling she had to do something, so she sold the land to McCabe Properties. Even after two years she was still sick about it. Selling off bits and pieces of her home seemed the only way to survive. Kit sighed and stood from her desk.

Her place, Sage Brush, once a thriving twenty-five hundred acre cattle ranch was now only a smallholding of three hundred acres. The homestead to generations of proud Kendalls and as far as Kit was concerned it would stay that way. She was not giving up yet. She'd be hanged if Sage Brush were lost under her watch.

Kit started to leave her office, just as her younger sister, Macy, stuck her red head in the doorway.

"Hey, don't forget. You're taking me to church in the morning. That new boy, Johnny Duke, is going and I want to get there early."

"Okay. But why are you telling me this now?"

"I'm going over to Becky's. We're giving each other manicures. Gotta run."

Kit blinked at her sister's dizzying departure. It would be nice to be fifteen again, without a care in the world.

The aroma of freshly baked bread drew Kit into the roomy kitchen. Maggie's tall angular form was just lowering the pan of hot yeast rolls onto the massive pine table. Kit shuffled in and slumped into one of the chairs. Maggie, the Kendalls' longstanding housekeeper and cook of thirty years wisely placed two hot rolls and a chunk of cold butter on a plate in front of her.

"Don't tell me, another cancellation?" Maggie asked.

"Yup." Kit tried to sound nonchalant, hoping to hide the fact that she was upset. She tore off an ample bite of bread and liberally buttered it before shoving the hot morsel between her lips.

"Oh goodness, that bad, huh?"

Kit glanced at Maggie and shook her head. "You always know, don't you?"

"Sugar, I'd have to be blind not to know."

"Honestly, Maggie, if these cancellations keep up, I'll have to sell." A sick feeling settled in the pit of Kit's stomach. Last month, she had seriously considered accepting their job offer as assistant manager. Had actually met with a representative from their corporate office in Dallas. Had even shaken hands on the deal. It was moments like this that she wondered if she'd made the right decision in turning it down, even if it did mean giving up more of her land.

"What'd the bank say?" Maggie grabbed the milk from the fridge and poured Kit a glass.

"Mr. Brown's working with me, but things aren't looking too good. He said it was far better to give up thirty acres, than to lose all three hundred in foreclosure." Kit took a sip of cold milk. "Needless to say, he was not pleased when I called to tell him I'd decided to turn the resort's offer down."

"I'm not surprised. They're not a mom and pop bank anymore." Maggie sprinkled flour on the mass of dough and pushed the rolling pin across its surface. "Now, don't go getting your hackles up, but maybe you should reconsider McCabe's job offer. To work at a fancy place like that and have no more headaches. I'm surprised you won't at least consider it."

"I have considered it, more than once. The extra money would supplement my income, allow me to pay the bills, and keep the B&B afloat." She ticked the reasons off on her fingers. "But, I just can't bring myself to sell more of Sage Brush, no matter how tempting the offer."

"I realize that, sugar, but seems to me it would be better than losing all your land to the bank? The resort only wants thirty acres."

"And most of it road frontage. Just so McCabe Resort can meet some codes issue. Something they should have thought about before expanding."

"You have plenty of road frontage."

"I know, and it's not even that really. It's just this blasted encroaching onto my property. When will it end?"

"Why not go on over there and tour the place like they suggested?" Maggie said. "If nothing else, it would be a good excuse to check out the competition."

"You sound like you want me to do this."

"Sugar, I just hate to see you struggling that's all. Taking a look means just that." Maggie patted Kit's shoulder and stood up. "What was the position they offered you?"

"Assistant Manager." The mere thought of such a lofty position at the lodge formerly owned by the man who had destroyed her father was tempting to say the least. Poetic justice served on a platter. At the time, sweet revenge had filled her senses like royal jelly to a queen bee. But when that vixen from Dallas told her the offer was contingent upon her selling them more of Sage Brush, all thoughts of her loan and the fact that she was two months delinquent on the payments, fled. She'd refused and hung up the phone.

Kit licked her buttery fingers, then wiped them on her napkin. "Since old man Dawson cut Sam out of his will, everybody's wondering who bought the lodge. You haven't heard, have you?"

"No sweetie, I haven't."

"I bet it's some big corporation out of Dallas or Houston," Kit pushed the bread across her plate, mopping up the last bit of butter. "Anyway, if I ever have to sell, at least if won't be to a Dawson."

"Sugar, you'd better watch that grudge. It'll eat you alive."

Kit hated to admit to it, but it was that very grudge that kept her going. It was the fuel to her fire. The driving force behind every decision she made with regard to Sage Brush. The very thought of the Dawsons made her anger-meter rise like a thermometer on a scorching hot day.

"Adam Dawson stole my family's land and as far as I'm concerned his son was a part of it," she said.

"You don't know that. Besides, I feel sorry for the boy, with his father cutting him out of his will and all. That lodge should have gone to Sam."

"That's your problem. You still think of him as a boy. The man is thirty years old."

"You sure came to that number mighty quick."

"We have the same birthday, as if you don't remember. Just about every cake you ever made for me had his name on it, too. Sam and Kit. You could have at least put my name first."

"Well, since he's six years older, I thought his name should be first."

Kit pushed back from the table. "Why are we even talking about him?"

"You brought him up. I didn't."

Kit went back to her desk to deal with the mail. One envelope in particular had been mocking her for the past two days. Better to just get it over with. She tore off the edge and slid out the bill. Her stomach plummeted.

She turned her attention to the vintage 1940's black phone sitting on her desk and wondered for the umpteenth time if she should call her mother, but decided against it. Kit now owned the B&B and worrying her mom, especially while she and Jeff were finally on their honeymoon, was out of the question. They'd waited over a year for this trip, and Kit wasn't about to spoil things for them now.

Daisy had wanted to sell the ranch after she'd remarried. Some lofty corporation had offered to buy the place. How her mother could even contemplate selling their homestead was beyond Kit. As she recalled, her mother had tried every logical argument she could think of to convince her, but Kit had stood firm, promising she could make a go of it. With her degree in hospitality and hotel management, she knew she could make it work. But that was before the hunting lodge was refurbished, reopening next door as the only five-star resort for miles.

Since then, it was all she could do to make ends meet. Her guest load had been cut in half and some weeks, since the resort re-opened, she didn't have any guests.

She eyed the past-due bank bill in her hand. Last year, she'd taken out a loan to update the bathrooms. It was only recently that she'd struggled to make those payments on time. Now she was two months behind and paying whatever she could scrape together.

Kit clutched the bill between her fingers and stared out the window at the sea of green just past the tennis courts. Maybe it wouldn't hurt to take a look.

Chapter 2

Sam drummed his fingers on the massive walnut desk that sat near the center of the airy office. Floor-to-ceiling windows opened to the well-groomed landscape that spread out before him letting in natural light that made working indoors a pleasure.

A sharp rap on the door brought him back to the present. "Come in."

"Sorry to disturb you, but I have some papers for you to sign." Sam's assistant, Diana DuPont, entered the room as she spoke.

"No you're not."

"Not what?"

"Sorry to disturb me," he drawled.

Diana's lips parted in her faultless smile. As usual, she was very well put together and near perfect. Dressed in a pale yellow silk suit that fit her beautifully, he couldn't help but admire her long legs and slender waist. She had the ability to dress feminine but professional, always maintaining a hint of haughty disdain. Giving her the ability to snub one second and flatter the next. In fact, he'd seen her venom spewed on more than one occasion and had warned her never to do it to any of his guests or acquaintances. She wasn't in Dallas anymore. But for all of that, she was the best assistant he'd ever had.

"The quarterly board meeting has been moved up and I've contacted everyone one the board to let them know. Anything else?"

"No, that's fine, thanks."

He finished signing the documents, then watched Diana's

hips sway as she left his office, certain she did it on purpose. Like a black widow spider in that respect. He'd seen her capture more than one unsuspecting male in her provocative web. Fortunately, he was immune.

After dropping Macy off a church, Kit pointed the truck toward the main highway and McCabe's Resort Lodge. The contrast between her B&B and the resort was unbelievable. One moment she was driving through dry parched ground and the next, lush green tropics. The resort had certainly put a crimp in her little bed and breakfast. A mere nuisance until they'd put in the golf course, which seemed to taunt her with its pristine, manicured greens splayed across the terrain like fingers. How they managed to keep the fairways green during the worst draught in fifty years was beyond her. She shook her head. A testament to modern irrigation, no doubt.

Pulling into the guest parking spot, she turned off the engine and gave herself one last pep talk. "This is a tour. I am not making a commitment." Assuming she'd have to meet with that citified vixen Diana DuPont again, she cringed, took a steadying breath, then jumped out of her truck.

The grounds were immaculate, beautifully displaying a mixture of local desert flora with colorful masses of hardy annuals and perennials. From her office window, McCabe's Lodge appeared green, but up close the foliage was breathtaking. How could she ever compete with this?

Kit followed the curve of the walkway to the front entrance, where a smiling bellman welcomed her by opening the massive doors with ease.

When she stepped into the grand foyer, she gasped. The interior was completely different from the rustic lodge she'd remembered. Glass and natural light were everywhere. Giant palms stood in front of long-paned windows. The original pine beams that spanned the vaulted ceiling were still there, gleaming with warmth that only came with age. The place was a blend of deer antler chandeliers and sparking crystal. Expensive area rugs covered the wide-planked floors. Fine southwestern oil paintings and bronze sculptures were displayed throughout the entire area. Someone had done a remarkable job marrying the all leather masculine décor, to the plush but comfortable surroundings that met her gaze.

As she stood, mouth gaping, an attractive young woman approached her. Kit glanced down at her brown pants and blue button-down shirt and realized she had underdressed for the tour. She felt unsophisticated and unfeminine next to this chic young woman.

"Hi, I'm Sharon Ward, one of the assistant managers here. You must be Kit Kendall."

"How could you tell?"

"You looked a little lost." Sharon smiled, revealing a dimple beside her mouth. "Plus, Diana told me what you looked like. She asked me to give you the tour this morning."

Kit could just imagine Diana's description of her. *She'll be the drab skinny one with no makeup and dressed like a man.*

Kit gave herself a mental shake and refocused. Relieved she didn't have to deal with Diana, she smiled back at the sparkling brown-eyed girl in front of her. "Nice to meet you, Sharon," she said, as they shook hands.

Kit followed Sharon through the spacious foyer where guests had gathered for afternoon tea. The aroma of freshly baked scones filled the air. The tinkling of teacups against saucers held a special magic against the rustic surroundings.

After the informal tour of the hotel and spa, Sharon invited Kit to join her for coffee. "We have a comfortable sitting area in the office down this hall to the left. By the way, the new CEO is finally here. The hotel has been buzzing since he arrived. Let's see if he's in his office. I'm sure he'd like to meet you."

"Oh, I wasn't planning to meet the CEO today."

"That's all right. He won't mind."

"Well, if you're sure we won't be disturbing him."

"Not at all. He's always available to his employees. His words. Not mine." Sharon smiled. "And he's the nicest guy. He grew up here."

"He what?"

As they rounded the corner, Kit halted in her tracks.

Sam Dawson stood across the hallway talking to Diana DuPont. Gone was the lanky twenty-four-year-old ranch hand she'd remembered. A sophisticated, well-dressed executive stood with confident authority in his stead. What was he doing here? He'd been cut from Adam's Dawson's will. What could possibly be his connection to McCabe Properties?

"Oh, good. There's Sam now. I'll introduce you."

Kit's stomach lurched. "Sharon, I'm sorry, but I have to go."

"Is everything all right?"

"Yes, I just remembered I have a doctor's appointment." She lied.

At that moment Sam turned his head and their eyes met, and held. Neither moved as they stared at each other. If eyes could take first place at the county fair, then his would win hands down. They were still the most remarkable blue she'd ever seen. Even from this distance, she could see every shade of the ocean. Glittering cobalt. Fathoms deep.

She used to drown in those eyes. But, never again.

Kit turned and fled.

Sam looked over at the slender form staring at him as if he'd had two heads. Then sudden realization dawned with such force, he swore under his breath.

Kit.

This was not how he'd planned to meet her again. On first glance, he'd thought the short-haired, freckle-faced kid staring at him was a boy. His heart skipped a beat.

What the heck happened to her?

Damn, this was awkward. The play of emotions that crossed Kit's face intrigued him. Her beautiful green eyes narrowed into slits, reminding him of a coiled rattler ready to strike.

He watched her stiffen and then spin like a top before she hurried down the corridor. The accusatory look in her green eyes had kept him rooted to the spot. Besides, he wasn't about to go chasing after her through his hotel. Dignity dictated it, if nothing else. He waited about five seconds before he excused himself from Diana. He walked coolly, deliberately, down the hallway. He saw Kit hurry out the front entrance just as he entered the reception area. Ignoring the bellman, he pushed through the front doors and then broke into a run.

"Kit. Wait!"

She didn't.

Max caught up with her just as she yanked frantically at the truck door handle. He grabbed hold of her arm.

Kit spun around, slapping at him with her hands. He let go of her and stepped back to give her some space. Holding her gaze, he stood patiently waiting for her to get under control. Panting from running, she reminded him of a trapped animal. He stared deep into her eyes. Although guarded and questioning, they still reminded him of a field of green clover on a sunny day. Her rosy lips parted and he wondered if they were still as sweet as he'd remembered them. He gave himself a mental shake and a good talking-to. Now was not the time to reminisce over old times in the hayloft. Standing before him was a coiled spring and he wanted to give her time to calm down.

He watched her, acutely aware of each ragged inhale and the rise and fall of her breasts. The last time he saw her, her hair was long cords of shinny copper. He used to love the way it shimmered around her shoulders in that little cotton dress she always wore. That green polka dot thing that made her eyes sparkle, like emeralds. Now, her hair seemed darker, probably because it was so short, but he knew if he touched it, the strands would still feel like silk in his hands.

Who the heck had butchered her hair, and that outfit? And he'd thought nothing had changed around here. When he noticed her breaths were coming slow and steady, he spoke.

"Are you okay?"

Kit nodded.

A slight smile curved his lips. "Hello, Kit." He placed his hand on the hood of the 1958 Chevy truck. "I see you're still driving the old girl."

Kit glanced briefly at her red truck, then turned her attention back to Sam. "What are you doing here?"

Her voice trembled, and he felt a sudden tug against his ribs.

"I was going to let you know I was back. I'm sorry you had to stumble on me like this."

"But, I thought, everyone thought—"

"That my father cut me out of his will?"

Kit nodded.

He smiled. He was in no hurry to fill her in on the details. "You know, I remember you as more of a talker."

Kit pursed her lips together. "So, you *weren't* cut out of his will."

"Right to the point, as always." He stuffed his hands into his pockets. "Yes, he did cut me out. But now is not the time, nor the place, to discuss it. I have more pressing things to talk over with you. I'm meeting with the board of directors in two days and I'd like to know why you backed out of the sale."

Kit stiffened. "I didn't back out of anything."

Sam folded his arms across his chest. "Really? Then what do you call it when someone commits to a deal then pulls out at the last minute? Or, does the Kendall word no longer mean anything?"

"That sale was contingent upon me working here. Look, I don't have to explain anything to you." Kit jerked open the truck door and clamored in. "I have something to say all right, but I'll save it for the owner of McCabe Properties."

Sam watched Kit put the truck in gear and drive away. He used to love driving that truck. A vision of Kit tucked up next to him as he shifted gears invaded his thoughts. He rubbed his hand across his jaw. He was tempted to tell her right then and there that he *was* McCabe Properties. But somehow he knew that information would hurt her deeply. He figured she'd seen his being cut from his father's will as a form of punishment for what he'd done to her. Well, he'd let her go on thinking it, at least for a day or two. He needed that road frontage. If he didn't get it, his investors would lose a fortune, half the people he'd already committed to hiring would lose their jobs, and Kit would lose everything.

Chapter 3

Maggie entered the living room with a broad smile on her face, carrying a tray with coffee and a small bowl of fruit. "Lunch is almost ready."

"What's up with you? Win the lottery or something?"

"Pete's on his way home. He's got two weeks before his summer session at Texas A&M."

"He's coming back early. How was roundup?"

Maggie beamed and took a seat next to Kit. "He said he had the time of his life."

"They always say that after their first. Just wait 'til it's his real job."

"Have you heard from Macy yet?"

"Only once. She texted me after she got on the bus. She was sitting next to that new kid, Johnny Duke, so she was in heaven." Kit pulled a face.

Maggie poured Kit a hot cup, added ample cream and sugar and handed it to her, then fixed her own. "Do I detect sarcasm in that sweet voice of yours?"

"You do," Kit took a sip, then slumped back against the sofa cushion.

"I swear, you could use a Johnny Duke in your life."

"I've had my Johnny Duke, thank you. No need to burst Macy's bubble, though. She'll find out how men are soon enough."

"Honey, your problem is, you just haven't met the right man."

The sudden image of aquamarine eyes hit Kit right between hers.

Maggie sipped on her coffee and gazed out the window. "I still can't believe it. I just can't believe it."

Kit groaned. "You've been saying that for two days."

"I wonder how long he's been back?" Maggie asked.

Kit shrugged, then plucked a green grape off the cluster she held in her hand and popped it into her mouth.

"So, except for Sam bowling you over, how *was* the competition?"

"Lord, Maggie, you should see the place. I don't see how we'll ever keep up." Kit propped both feet on the coffee table in front of her. "It's really remarkable. Very modern yet rustic." She jammed two more grapes into her mouth.

"Hmm, sounds real nice."

"It's fabulous." She let out a heavy sigh.

"I guess you won't be taking the job." Maggie reached into the ceramic bowl and gently snipped off a plump grape.

"Of course, I'm not. No way am I parting with more of my property. Besides, even if I wanted to, I could never work for Sam."

"What do you mean, work for him?"

"He's obviously running the place."

"I see what you mean." Maggie said, then popped off a small cluster. "Sure is a heck of a lot of money, though. And for thirty acres, too. They must be up to something."

"Exactly."

"You know, if you could bring yourself to let it all go, I bet these McCabe folks would buy the whole place. Then you'd have enough to buy that little B&B in Carter's Creek and then some."

"If this wasn't generations of Kendall land, believe me, I would."

"Could they be the same company that wanted to buy the place from your mama, a while back?"

Kit sat up straighter. "Could be, I guess."

"I wonder how he got the head job? Sounds like he finagled that one." Maggie chuckled. "If anyone could finagle, it was Sam. You're sure he told you he was cut from his daddy's will?"

"Yes, he stood right there in the parking lot and told me so himself."

Kit turned toward the shiny new truck coming up the drive and slow to a stop.

"Wonder who that could be?" Maggie asked.

They stood and watched Sam climb out of the black vehicle.

Kit shook her head and couldn't help but snort. "He'll have a time keeping the dust off that. But he always did go against the grain. And look at him, all spiffed up in a suit, no less. Six years away, and you'd think he'd never lived here. It's disgusting."

"Are you plum crazy? I've never seen a more handsome young man. A real gentleman. Why, my Pete doesn't even hold up to that."

Sam strode up the steps and knocked.

Maggie rushed to open the screen door. "Heavens above. As I live and breathe, it's Sammy Dawson. I couldn't believe it when Kit said you'd come back. It's about time you came to see me."

"Maggie, you haven't changed a bit." Sam's eyes crinkled at the corners as he wrapped his strong arms around her. "Boy, have I missed you."

"You mean you've missed my steak biscuits." She chuckled, giving him a big Texas hug in return.

Kit leaned back against the massive bow front cabinet and folded her arms across her chest. She shook her head as she watched Maggie slobber all over him.

"And your *cow patties*," Sam continued, referring to Maggie's enormous oatmeal pecan chocolate chip cookies.

"You haven't changed either, sugar pie. You could always smell them as you were coming up the drive."

Sam threw back his head and laughed.

Kit caught her breath. His handsome face lit up and her heart thudded in treacherous response. She suffered an intense longing as she watched him place a masculine arm across Maggie's shoulder, reminding her of the comfortable intimacy they'd once shared. Awakening feelings she'd tried for years to forget.

Dropping her gaze, she pretended to brush something off her blouse as Maggie led Sam back to the living room. Sheer longing spread to Kit's very core as she followed behind them. She hated that he could still make her *feel*. Anger flared in her gut. He had a lot of nerve showing up here like nothing had changed. Clamping her lips together, she perched her bottom on the edge of her desk while Maggie quickly excused herself.

"Well, that's a sight to see," Kit said, watching the tall, angular woman bustle off to the kitchen.

"What is?"

"Maggie. Flitting," Kit said, waving her hands in the air.

"You mean she doesn't *flit* for you?"

She turned her attention back to Sam, startled by the twinkle in his eyes.

She raised her chin a notch. "Not usually." Her instinct was to slide off the desk, but instead she calmly unfolded her arms and placed her palms on the desk. She cocked her brow in his direction, hoping like the devil her thudding heart would not give her true feelings away. She gazed at his face, amazed at how little had changed. The five-o'clock shadow defined his square jaw and accented his firm lips. She deliberately raked her eyes up and down his navy blue suit.

"You going to a funeral?" But before he could answer, Maggie burst back in with a plate of cookies.

"You will stay for lunch, won't you?" Maggie asked.

Since when do we have cookies before lunch? Kit slid off the desk in a rush to give Maggie the eye, which she either didn't notice or deliberately chose to ignore.

"Sam can't stay. He's going to a funeral."

"Actually, I've already been to a funeral, of sorts. McCabe Properties' board meeting." He smiled.

Kit held her breath and turned back toward him. Just as she thought he was going to decline, he glanced at her. Something, she chalked up as innate orneriness, crossed his handsome features.

"Actually," he drawled. "A good meal amongst friends is exactly what I need."

Steaming, Kit followed behind them. When she entered the kitchen she watched in amazement as he pulled out a straight back chair and settled his long frame comfortably at the table.

Maggie, clucking over him like some broody hen, was the last straw.

"Don't set a place for me." Kit blurted out. "I've got work to do," Glaring at both of them, she slammed out the back door and headed for the tack room.

Kit hung two bridles and a harness on the three-pronged stainless steel hook hanging from the tack room ceiling determined to ignore the occasional laughter wafting from the house. Squaring her shoulders, she grabbed a bar of saddle soap and got to work. After she soaped up a sponge, she began cleaning out the pores in the leather, releasing the faint scent of avocado and bees wax. Getting the dirt out took some elbow grease and that plus the ninety-degree heat made her dripping wet in minutes. Sweat tickled her neck while she soaped up another six-inch section of the harness. If the soap turned gray she had to clean the area again.

She slugged through this process, piece by piece, wiping the leather clean after each scrubbing. Laughter drifted from the house. Again. Kit clenched her teeth and jerked the sponge over the bridle, nicking her finger. "Oww! Dang it!" She slapped her finger against her lips, and sucked. Would he ever leave? She glanced at her watch. She'd been out here for forty-five minutes. *How long does it take one man to eat lunch? Doesn't he have things to do? Shouldn't he be at the resort? Working?* She moistened the rag, slid it over the rein, and pulled. Maybe she should report him to McCabe Properties. She grinned. Would she love getting him in trouble, or what?

Kit cocked her head to one side. Finally. They'd stopped talking. Hopefully Sam was gone. Hanging the bridle next to the others, she left the barn, vowing to throw him out if need be.

Hot peppered roast beef wafted from the stove as she entered the back door. Her stomach growled. Thankful the kitchen was empty, she ladled an ample amount of beef stew into a bowl, cut herself a wedge of cornbread, and then sat down to eat. As she put the spoon to her lips, she froze.

Sam's laughter rang out from the living room.

Chapter 4

The swinging door flew open and if Sam hadn't know better, he'd have sworn it was a bull busting out of its pen.

He knew he could outlast Kit, always could. Knew it was only a matter of time before she reappeared on the scene. Kit was never one to be left out of things.

"Oh, there you are," Maggie, said. "We've been having the best chat. Did you know Sam still owns the lodge next door? Isn't that wonderful?"

Kit's eyes grew wide as saucers and the blood drained from her sun-kissed complexion, taking all but the freckles from her face. She ran her feminine, shaking hands over the top of her head causing several silky red spikes to stand on end. She opened her mouth to speak, but not a peep emerged.

He watched her dusty jean-clad body sway and just as he was about to jump to his feet to assist her, she collapsed into a nearby chair. She swallowed hard and raised her misty green eyes to his face. With bated breath, he watched shock turned to outrage as Kit's expressive eyes turned dark with anger. Kit had always been one of the most open, readable women he knew. He wondered if she was aware of it.

"Maggie, you haven't forgotten about the eats for tomorrow's barn raising, have you?" Kit asked in a tightly controlled voice.

"Good gracious, I sure have." She glanced at the wall clock and then stood.

Sam rose with Maggie and received her hug.

"We're so glad you're back home, hon." Maggie said.

He smiled at her and didn't say anything until she'd left the room. "She's a wonderful woman."

He lowered his body back into the club chair. "We both missed you at lunch. You really shouldn't hurt her feelings just because I'm here."

"Then don't show up uninvited."

Kit sat up straight, shoulders back, all fight and sass and met his gaze. Staring at him without so much as a blink. Except for her outward appearance he was happy to see she hadn't changed all that much. Most people would after losing land, position, and the finer things in life - a fact that didn't seem to bother this feisty young woman who sat before him.

"So, you're the owner." She said.

"Yes. I am."

"I don't know why I'm surprised. I'm sure like your father, you swindled somebody."

Sam clenched his jaw. It took every ounce of restraint not to shoot from the chair. Instead, he stood slowly and gave her a look that pinned her to the seat.

"The land was my mother's, Kit. McCabe land. It never belonged to my father. And if I were you, I'd be thanking God I'm a man with self-control."

She barely cringed but the rosy flush to her cheeks and the slight flutter of her eyelids told him he'd hit his mark.

"Oh." She shrank back slightly and sank deeper into her chair.

"You can think what you'd like. Right now, I don't really care. But there are at least fifty people in Sugar Creek who are depending on me for work. Many of them you know."

"Well, because of you, *I've* had to fire two of my guides."

"I'm sorry for that, but don't blame your bad business decisions on me. Work with me, and everybody has a job. Don't, then you will lose everything."

Kit's rosy cheeks paled to a ghostly white. He hadn't meant to say that. Hadn't meant to take it that far.

"What are saying?" Kit stood to her feet. "You dare to threaten me?"

"Look, Kit, you can either be a part of the solution, one that meets both of our needs or not. It's up to you. You either sell to me, or I'll have no other choice but to go to Plan B. And I'm telling you right now, you won't like it."

She raised her chin a fraction and tossed her red head back like a mare ready to spring forward in a race. He remembered that move, the way she tossed her head before speaking her mind. Her copper mane used to tumble like fire around her flawless complexion. But now the action only resulted in a slight bounce of short copper layers across her forehead.

"Your threats hold no weight with me, Sam Dawson."

He folded his arms across his chest. "It's no threat. I have investors and shareholders to answer to. Frankly, you could use a good dose of accountability, yourself. At least someone would be around to stop you from making a mess of things." He turned, grabbed his Stetson off the hall table, and with a coolness he was far from feeling, settled it on his head. In three strides, he was out the door.

Kit watched Sam cross the front yard to his truck, then closed the front door. She leaned back against the solid wood and released her breath. Her heart pounded against the massive oak panel behind her. What did he mean she could lose everything? And how could he own the place if his father cut him out of the will? It didn't make sense. Brushing angrily at the hot tears coursing down her cheeks, she pushed away from the door and went to the kitchen.

She found Maggie peeling a pan of potatoes. "The nerve of him, showing up after all these years, and waltzing in here after what his family has done."

"Humph, I thought something was up with you." Maggie stood, ramrod straight, at the sink. "What your mama would say if she were here—"

"Well, she's not."

"Have you even talked to Sam? Found out his side?"

"Talk to him? I haven't seen the man for six years. Or, heard from him," she finished lamely, then plopped in a kitchen chair.

"Then all the more reason." Maggie shook her gray head. "I swear. It's no wonder you're off men with an attitude like that. It would do you good to take some pointers from your little sister."

"Maggie. Do you really expect me to flit around like Macy? Like I'm still fifteen and full of myself?"

Maggie wiped her hands on her apron and sat down next to Kit. "Of course not, but just because you run a B&B ranch doesn't mean you have to look like a boy, you know. Look at you. Hair chopped off—"

"It's easier this way." Kit ran a hand over her short hair.

"And, you smell like horses half the time. Grow out that gorgeous red hair of yours. Put on one of those little cotton sun dresses you used to wear." Maggie placed a hand on Kit's shoulder. "You have nothing to prove, you know."

Actually, she did. Kit stood abruptly to her feet, scraping her chair over the wide, planked floors.

"All the same, I will not have you giving him cow patties or hot biscuits or anything else from this kitchen."

"Careful, sugar pie, or you'll be eating those words."

Bright and early Saturday morning, Kit dragged herself out of bed and to the neighbor's. The Miller's barn raising party was under way and the entire town had turned out for the event.

Including Sam. It'd been five days since he'd walked out of her house. Not that she was counting. It took all of Kit's inner strength not to stare at him but that's not to say she didn't look. Feasted, was more like it. Shirtless and sweaty, Sam's taut muscles glistened under the afternoon sun. Shaking her head, she willed her mind to stay focused on the task in front of her.

Maggie sat next to her under a shade tree at a long table, handing out steak biscuits, potato salad, and sweet iced tea to those taking a break from work.

Kit looked up, ready to had out another plate, to find Sam standing all tight T-shirted and masculine right in front of her. Even though he'd put his shirt back on the sweat had plastered it tightly across his chest. As he accepted the plate, her fingers brushed against his, shooting tingling sensations down to her toes. She stared up at him and her heart raced, tapping out the all too familiar *rata-tat-tat* that used to make her heart sing. Why didn't he leave? What the heck was he standing there for?

She continued to stare at him, mesmerized by the tiny beads of sweat trickling down his bronze neck.

"I'd sure like a cold drink, if you don't mind."

Kit blinked and realized he was waiting for her to grab an iced tea from the drink table stationed behind her. Turning swiftly, she grabbed the drink, then carefully placed it in his free hand. She watched him stride away to sit with a group of men at a nearby picnic table.

"How do those words taste now, sugar?" Maggie gave Kit her 'older and wiser' smile.

Kit glared at Maggie, then served the next guy in line.

Sam watched Kit fix a plate and settle herself beneath an oak tree. Just as she chomped down on an ample piece of steak biscuit, he appeared at her side.

"Mind if I join you?" He had timed the question just as her mouth was full so she'd be less likely to say 'no'. But the darts shooting from her eyes told him exactly what her mouth could not. He ignored it and sat down next to her. Sunlight dappled through the leaves that canopied over them, sparking fire off the copper strands that covered her head.

Kit scooted her rear over in an attempt to put some distance between them. "Yes, I mind," she finally got out after practically choking on her food. "Besides, won't your Dallas friend miss you?"

"Diana? She's a big girl. I'm sure she'll be fine for a few minutes without me." He gazed at Diana who stood across the yard, preening and smiling at small group of men gathered around her."

He glanced back at Kit. She was eyeing Diana and her entourage with something close to repugnance.

"What a flirt. And that dress. Dang. Was she poured into it?" Kit fingered a button on her baggy checked blouse. "How do you stand it? She's like a mare in season."

He threw back his head and laughed. "I still see you have a way with words."

"Just trying to keep you grounded." She cleared her throat. "I have to say, I never figured you with someone like her."

"You mean someone, long-legged and gorgeous?"

Kit forked a potato wedge. "Just sayin."

"I don't know? I went for you didn't I?" He dove into his dessert, deliberately changing the subject. "This pie is great. Maggie's?"

"As if you don't know," she said, pulling a face.

He couldn't help but smile at her expression. "Boy, do I remember that look."

Kit shrugged her slender shoulders and he wondered if they were still as smooth and golden brown as he remembered them. Hard to tell in that worn out shirt she had on. A shirt that was clearly a size too big for her. It hung on her like a flour sack.

He finished off the pie and leaned back against the tree. "How's Macy?"

Kit's green eyes sparkled like gems, holding him spellbound for a brief moment. He hadn't seen that candid expression in her eyes since he'd returned.

"She's great." Kit dropped her gaze to the plate in her lap.

Good, he'd found a safe topic. "I guess she's all grown up now."

"Yep. She's fifteen. A real beauty, too. Silky red hair, no freckles."

"Sounds like she has changed. Which is to be expected, I guess."

"A lot happens to a girl between ten and fifteen," Kit toyed with a piece of biscuit on her plate.

"And beyond. Take you, for instance. You've grown up, too."

Kit's head whipped around at his words.

As a girl, Kit had followed Sam around on her horse helping him check and mend fences. He remembered how she'd struggled to hold the boards while he hammered them in place. Tough as nails, she'd never once complained. Unlike her father, who in his later years lived life with a bottle of whiskey in one hand and a deck of cards in the other.

"Except you still have freckles."

Kit's fingers flew to cover her nose.

He chuckled. "You know, I've never understood why you hate them. Frankly, that smattering of gold dust across your nose always enchanted me."

"I'm not selling, Sam, so you can forget all that sweet talk. It won't work with me."

"It used to." He tried like the dickens not to smile, but he did anyway. Then, sobering, he asked, "What happened to you, Kit? Why do you insist on carrying the weight of the world on your shoulders?"

"Who says I want to?" She rounded on him.

He watched her eyes smolder. Anxiety and anger replacing her former candidness.

"You shouldn't believe everything you hear," she said. "Most of it's fabricated." She jabbed her fork in the potato salad.

"And you should take your own advice."

"What does that mean?"

"Stop holding what my father did against me. We have a chance to begin again, without either one of them in our lives."

Her pretty mouth clamped shut. She lowered her eyes to the ground. Sam waited for the mouthy remark he was certain was coming. Instead, he watched her eyes widen in terror. She sprang to her feet.

He shot up beside her. "What is it?"

"Ants!" Ragged, raw fear ripped from Kit's throat.

Sam snatched her aside, then stomped the ground where she'd been sitting.

Kit grabbed his arm. "It's okay. I thought they were fire ants."

"I did, too." He said.

"What is this, some new spin on the Texas two-step?" Diana sauntered up, looking all powdered and perfect in her white sundress.

Sam met Kit's eyes met for what seemed an eternity before turning his attention to Diana.

"Sam, do you have a minute? Someone wants to meet you," Diana linked her arm through his.

"Of course." Despite his reluctance, he allowed himself to be led away by the Dallas beauty, leaving Kit to stare after them.

Kit turned down the thermostat, then joined Maggie in the kitchen. "That should cool things off a bit."

"Today was a scorcher, that's for sure," Maggie said.

"Having a barn raising on the same day as our chuck

wagon dinner makes for a long day. Are you sure you won't let me make the biscuits for tomorrow's breakfast?" Kit stretched her arms over her head.

"And since when has a long day ever stopped me?" Maggie poured buttermilk in the mixing bowl.

Kit laughed. "Never."

"Besides, I don't have to make near as many with such a small group. It's almost not worth having Sage Brush open for this few," Maggie sprinkled flour on the table in preparation for the dough.

"I know." Kit sighed, then lifted the lid to the old-fashioned glass cookie jar and pulled out a cow patty. "And it's only getting worse. Next week we don't have anybody." She nibbled the cookie. "If this keeps up I'll have to let someone else go."

"Not Jake. His wife's expecting their fourth. And Trip's just gotten married. That'd be a sorry way to start life with a new bride."

"You're not helping me any."

"Oh, don't mind me. You know how I ramble on. At least you don't have to decide anything right now."

Kit left Maggie to her task, and strode to the barn. Astride Pepper, she made her way across the back paddocks onto Lowman's land. Ever since her father had lost the bulk of his land to Allan Dawson, Susan Lowman, Lord bless her, had always allowed the Kendalls and their guests to camp and hunt on her property. Six years ago, the Dawsons acquired most of the Kendalls' property but there was one strip of Kendall land that still connected to the Lowman's, allowing her the access needed for her B&B to continue.

Kit entered the campsite, reined in, and walked Pepper over to the makeshift corral that Trip and Jake had set up near the trees. She greeted her guests with a smile and shook hands with several of them before positioning herself behind one of the hay bales that had been set out as seating. Trip sat nearby strumming his ukulele, leading the group of families in campfire songs. She studied the happy, contented faces and watched them sing. This was a scene straight from her childhood. Frankly, she couldn't remember not experiencing it. A pang shot through her heart. Would this be one of the last times Sage Brush would host such an evening? It was in her blood—the songs, the camaraderie, the horses. What she knew and loved. And just for the moment, she lost herself in the music and the stars up above.

Her gaze roamed over the group and rested on Trip's new bride, Tess. She watched her smiling, upturned face that literally glowed from the light of the campfire. Definitely the face of a young woman in love. It would be a real shame to have to let Trip go. The muscles in her stomach tightened. She clutched the buttons on her shirt as a wave of sickness engulfed her like a swarm of bees. *Don't think about it.* Kit took a deep breath, then slowly exhaled, focusing on the smiling faces around the campfire.

She turned and made her way across the rugged ground to where the horses stood swishing their tails. Gathering Pepper's reins, she grabbed hold of the leather horn, placed her booted foot in the stirrup, then settled herself in the saddle. As she headed back toward the house, the beginning chords of "Happy Trails" accompanied her departure. Trip always led the guests in that song on the last night. Kit wondered if they'd ever meet again. She certainly hoped so.

Chapter 5

Sunday morning, Kit waved her last guest goodbye, then helped Maggie carry the rest of the breakfast dishes into the kitchen. Normally, she was at church teaching her Sunday school class but since the girls were away at camp she was able to stay and help Maggie.

"What a great week."

"Yes, siree, those are mighty fine folks. One of the nicest groups we've had in a while."

"One of the only groups we've had in a while," Kit muttered as she began wiping off the counter. "I guess I'll see you at the end of the week. There're only four men coming, mainly to hunt and fish. Jake and his oldest boy are going to take them out, so I'll only need you to strip the beds and handle breakfast."

Kit and Maggie had worked out this alternate schedule since their guest list had shrunk over the past month.

"You know, I don't mind coming back earlier."

"Nope. You don't need to. I've got some rotten fence posts that need my attention. So, I'll be out of the house for a few days."

"Okay, there are plenty of leftovers in the fridge, so make sure to pack yourself lunch before you go traipsing all over hell's half acre."

"Yes, ma'am." Kit smiled fondly at her doting housekeeper/cook. She couldn't help but think of the day she'd pitched a fit with her mother about letting her keep Sage Brush and making a go of it. Her mom had finally agreed if Maggie would stay on and help. Which, she did.

"See you at the end of the week, sugar."

That evening, Kit drove over to Wayside Baptist Church for the Sunday night service. The traditional red brick building sat on the corner of North and Main, right in the center of town, its white steeple a welcoming beacon to all.

Kit waved to Maggie and her husband, then slipped into the oak pew about halfway back in the church. The message was on conquering giants, based on the Old Testament David and Goliath story.

Worried about her own looming giant, Kit listened with an open heart. The potential loss of Sage Brush had become a constant threat. As she thought about the upcoming property taxes, a knot formed in the pit of her stomach. The frightening reality was that even with full occupancy her mother had struggled to pay the taxes last year. Truth was, she needed a miracle. As she listened, she knew, just like David, the only way to defeat her giant was to use all of the resources she had at her disposal and then trust God with the rest.

After the service it was customary for everyone to meet in the fellowship hall for refreshments. She entered the room to the sounds of laughter and chairs scraping tile. Families and friends sat or stood in groups, while young children romped about with half-eaten cookies clutched in their little fists.

She helped herself to lemonade and a chocolate chip cookie, then joined a group of friends across the room. Susan Lowman, her daughter, Elizabeth, Trip, and Tess were comfortably seated and in the middle of a conversation when she joined them.

"I think it's wonderful how he's trying to bring this town back to life." Elizabeth paused to sip her lemonade.

"I swear, even the sidewalks look cleaner since his arrival." This brought a chuckle from the little group.

Kit forced a smile and turned her head to look at the man in question. Sam. He was leaning one muscular shoulder against the wall and smiling at something Jake was saying. He threw back his head in laughter. It was just as she'd remembered. Deep, vibrant and rich. Had it been anyone other than Sam, that laughter would have made her heart thump with a longing to know the man behind it. But she knew the man behind it and he was nothing like what that laughter promised. Once, she'd thought he was wonderful but that was then and this was now. No way would she get pulled into his outward charm and attractive cowboy looks. Not this time. She knew better. She was older and wiser to the likes of a Dawson. She turned away and focused on the group in front of her and something Susan Lowman was saying.

"At first, I was a bit concerned about selling land that's been in the Lowman family for generations. But frankly, it'd become a burden to take care of it. Oh, I'll keep the house and the south quadrant for a while but with Elizabeth engaged and moving to California"—Susan looked tenderly at her daughter— "and insisting that I go with her, well, what can I say? I feel good about my decision."

Kit caught and held her breath. Her stomach lurched as if a swarm of butterflies had taken up residence there.

"Mama, you're not supposed to talk about it yet," Elizabeth smiled fondly at her mother.

"I know, dear, but we're among friends. It's all right. But my daughter's right, we can't mention the sale to anyone else."

Kit exchanged glances with Trip. "But, Miss Susan, what about my access to your property? What about my guests?"

"Don't worry about that, dear. I'm sure he'll let you use the land.

"He?"

"Speak of the devil." Elizabeth chuckled and whispered under her breath.

Kit turned to see Sam approach, his smile wreaking havoc on her already confused senses.

Sam greeted everyone, shaking hands with Trip and Tess and congratulating them on their recent marriage. He sat down and turned his attention to Susan. "You look charming this evening," he said, a teasing light in his blue eyes.

Miss Susan flushed in delight.

Kit's eyes widened. A kick in her stomach wouldn't have hurt any more than this. Susan Lowman had sold her land to him. He had worked his damned Dawson charm on her and bought her land, sealing Kit's fate and the demise of Sage Brush for good. She couldn't believe it. Thank God she was seated. Her legs began to shake. If she'd tried to stand, she'd have fallen flat on her face. Overwhelmed, she sat there and watched as he laughed and talked with her friends. Poor Trip. He had no idea that he'd probably just lost his job, his livelihood. Where would he go? And Jake? With three kids and one on the way, would he have to go, too?

Suddenly she couldn't breath. The room grew darker. What was happening to her? Then everything went black.

Something cool pressed against her cheek and then her forehead. Her eyes fluttered open. What was Sam saying?

"Kit. Can you hear me?"

Sam held her against his chest. His heart beat strong, powerful thuds against her ear like distant thunder. She felt so safe, so secure. She wanted it to be like it was before he'd left. Before she knew him for the scoundrel he really was. Just a few more seconds. If only . . .

She opened her eyes and stared into blue pools of

concern. "I'm okay." She placed her hands against his firm chest and pushed herself out of the security of those powerful arms. God, how she still ached for him.

"Here, sip on this." Trip's wife, Tess, lifted a glass of water to Kit's lips.

Sam helped her to her feet, steadying her before letting her go.

"We'll take you home," Trip said.

"No, I'll take her. I'm right next door," Sam spoke with authority and no one, darn it, even thought about challenging him.

"It's okay, I'm all right. I can drive."

Sam laid his arm over Trip's shoulder, whispered something then turned back to Kit. "Fine, I'll walk you out." He took hold of Kit's elbow and led her through the fellowship hall. She tried to pull her arm out of his hold but he held tightly.

They went outside to where she'd parked her Chevy. As soon as Kit got the keys from her purse, Sam quickly slipped them right out of her hands.

"Hey, give those back?" He placed her keys on top of the front left tire of her truck. "Trip will get your truck home."

"I'm driving myself."

"No, you're not."

Kit sucked in her breath and glared up at him. "I don't want you to take me home. I don't want you anywhere near me."

Sam brushed his hand through his hair a. "Look, you can either walk to my truck or I'll carry you. Either way, I'm taking you home. It would be irresponsible of me to let you drive after what just happened. What if you fainted again?"

Kit stood her ground for as long as she deemed reasonable. She had no doubt that he'd carry out his threat, and as church members were starting to stream into the parking lot, she decided to let him have his way. This time.

She followed him to his truck and climbed in, deliberately refusing his helping hand.

Sam could tell she was spitting mad. He watched her jerk the seatbelt over her chest several times before he reached over to click it into place.

He straightened up and glanced at her as he turned into the street. "Is that steam I see coming from your ears?"

Kit responded by snapping her arms across her chest.

He heaved a sigh and shook his head. "She told you, didn't she?"

Kit didn't say a word she just stared out the window.

"I'm sorry you had to find out that way. I was going to stop by tonight and tell you myself."

"How thoughtful of you. So. What do you want?"

"Sorry?"

"For access to the land. Otherwise my guests have no place to hunt or fish."

"Sell me the road frontage I need." He'd deliberately forced her hand and hated himself for it. But far better for her to part with a few measly acres than lose everything. And if she ended up hating him in the process then so be it. He cursed both their fathers under his breath.

Kit's mouth fell open and she slowly turned to face him, hoarse laughter tumbling from her lips.

"You've got to be kidding. After this stunt, do you really think I'd sell an inch of my property to you? One Kendall made the mistake of caving to a Dawson's blackmail, but let me assure you, this one won't."

He hated what he was about to do. Hated to force her hand, but she gave him no choice. When did she become so stubborn? Gritting his teeth, he continued.

"Then I won't allow you to use the Lowman property for access. You'll be forced to shut down. Sage Brush will close. You'll be through. You'll lose your property to the bank when they foreclose. Then it'll only be a matter of time before I have it all anyway. Is that really what you want?"

"Why you no good, conniving, lowlife."

"Look at it this way, if I get the road frontage I need, then you get to stay in business. It's a win-win."

They slowed to a stop outside of her house.

Kit opened the truck door then turned to face him.

"You would actually do that? You'd put Trip and Jake out of work? And what about Maggie? Have you even thought of her?"

"I told you, you wouldn't like it."

Chapter 6

Kit got up at dawn. Sleeping in was never an option, even on those days when she had no guests. She fixed coffee and scrambled eggs while fighting the dark cloud that hovered over her. Ten minutes later, with dishes rinsed and in the sink, she made her way to the paddock. Shoulders hunched, she saddled Pepper and rode out of the compound. By midmorning, she'd checked every inch of her boundary line that touched what used to be Lowman's land. She'd hoped there might be a way to enter the south quadrant that still belonged to Miss Susan but there was none. Disappointed, she and Pepper made their way to her small cabin on the far corner of her property.

She dismounted near the water trough and secured the reins over the paddock railing. After pumping enough water for Pepper to have a drink, she entered the shed to get her beloved horse a snack. The aroma of sweet apple pie drifted upward from inside the galvanized can. Kit grabbed the last handful of dried apples making a mental note to bake more. Years ago, Sam had taught her to make dried apples to leave out at the run-in sheds as treats for the horses. He'd also taught her to keep single-size pop-a-top cans of applesauce on hand. Perfect for adding something sweet to crimped oats and pellet feed.

"There you go, girl." Kit opened her hand and Pepper lower her head. She never tired of the tickling sensation of Pepper's lips against her palm.

After their short break, they made their way back to the homestead. She still had roughly three hundred acres, which was enough for trail rides and chuck wagon dinners, but unless the mule deer or the pig-like javelina wandered onto her land, and the river changed course, certainly not enough for hunting and fishing. She thought about the four men scheduled to hunt javelina next week and realized she'd better find out when Sam was closing on the Lowman property. Hopefully, she wouldn't have to cancel her guests. It would be tough if she had to refund their deposit, especially since she'd already spent most of it.

She entered the yard, unsaddled Pepper, and released her in the paddock. Sticky with sweat and dust, Kit stepped onto the back porch. Balancing on one foot, she pulled off one boot and then the other. Next, she wriggled out of her jeans, yanking them from her legs with a stubborn jerk. Sweat trickled down her back plastering her shirt to her skin. Anticipating a cool shower, she peeled off her T-shirt. Just as she bent over to gather up the dusty clothes, she heard someone clear his throat from behind.

Kit spun around, her eyes wide as saucers. *Sam!* "What the heck are you doing here?" She gathered the wad of clothes to her chest in a vain attempt to cover her partial nakedness.

She'd never stripped off her clothes in front of a man before, except for once on a dare and even then it'd only been her blouse. If the ground could have opened up right then and there, she would have been elated. Standing stock-still, her mind raced to find a way out. She knew if she turned to run inside, he'd see her dingy panties and bra from the back. She would rather die first. She took a step backward toward the door, but stopped, feeling like a complete fool. Oh God, he was laughing at her. The mirth in his blue eyes was unmistakable. That slight tilt of his lips had her heart thundering in her chest like wild horses galloping across the plains. He was insanely good looking, gorgeous, in fact, and what was worse, he knew it, too.

"What do you want?" she snapped.

That roguish grin, the one that used to haunt her dreams, slowly formed on Sam's handsome face. Lord, she used to lay awake at night thinking about that smile and the way it lit up his blue eyes, just like it did right now as he stood looking at her.

"You need any help?"

"What I need is for you to turn that horse around and ride out of here." Instead, he dismounted and ascended the steps. He stepped up onto the porch and looked down at her.

Riveted, Kit stared up into those blue diamonds, her eyes never leaving his face. Sam touched her cheek with the back of his hand, ratcheting Kit's heartbeat up a notch.

"I'll go around to the front door. You go ahead and get cleaned up." He glanced at the dusty clothes in her hands. "Unless you've moved the extra key, I'll go ahead and let myself in."

"It's not locked." Kit pressed her lips together and watched him lead his horse over to the paddock. When she was certain he wouldn't turn around, she hurried into the house.

After a quick shower, she slipped into a clean pair of jeans and sleeveless light blue shirt. Then gave her hair a quick brushing, and ran downstairs, where she found Sam sprawled out in what used to be her father's favorite chair.

Holding her head high, she entered the living room. *Play it cool, act mature.*

"Would you like something cold to drink, before I throw you out?"

His eyes still held a twinkle in their blue depths. "Sure." He stood and followed her to the kitchen. "I've never been thrown out before. I'm actually kind of looking forward to it. How will you manage it?"

Halfway to the kitchen, Kit glanced back and gave him the dirtiest look she could conjure up. Once in the kitchen, she watched Sam lean against the doorframe. She sucked in a sharp breath. She couldn't help it. It flat-out galled her to see him so relaxed and comfortable in her home. She felt his eyes on her as she opened the refrigerator to pour them both a glass of iced tea. Turning back to him, she stopped abruptly at the expression on his face.

"Ah, you got anything stronger?" he asked.

She clamped her lips together, then reached in for a beer. She held out the cold bottle of Shiner to him. "That better?"

"Immensely." Sam took the beer from her outstretched hand. "Let's go sit down," he said, retreating to the living room.

"You know, I wish you wouldn't give me orders in my own home." Kit sat down opposite him and sipped her tea. "So. When are you signing the papers? I have guests next week that are coming specifically to hunt javelina."

"Next month, on the twenty-seventh."

Kit glared at him. If her eyes were daggers, he'd be either wounded or dead by now. "Have you thought anymore about my proposition?"

"Since yesterday? No."

"Come on, Kit, I know you. You probably laid awake most of the night thinking about it."

She glowered at him. "Don't rush me." Kit crossed then uncrossed her legs. "I'm still thinking about it but I plan to get advice before I make any decision."

"From who?"

"Maggie, Trip, and Jake, for a start. I don't know, probably my mom."

"How is your mother? I heard she got married and is on an extended honeymoon."

"She did. And, yes, she'll be gone most of the summer."

"You don't sound too happy about it."

Kit raised her chin. "I am too, happy about it. He's a wonderful man. He was one of our guests several years ago. A widower. He came back every year to hunt until one visit when he just sort of hung around, helping mom out, stuff like that."

Kit's pink lips tilted upward and her eyes took on a subtle twinkle, landing him a one-two punch in his gut.

"It was cute, really. They were like high school sweethearts. He brought her flowers and candy. Took her dancing."

Her green eyes suddenly lit up like gems. A confident, contagious smile broke from her lips. It was the first time since he'd come back that she was her old self. All sparkly. In love with life. This was the Kit he knew. But then she must have realized that who she was talking to because she sobered. And just like that, the light went out and a frown clouded her features. He hated like hell that he did that to her. And if she didn't cooperate with him, things would only get worse.

"Daisy's a fine person. She deserves some happiness," he said.

"Kit stared at him. "Yes, she does, but not for the same reason you're thinking. She and my father loved each other. They were doing fine until . . ."

"Until my father destroyed him. Is that what you were going to say?"

"You said it, I didn't."

"You didn't have to. It's in your expressions, your bearing, your eyes. You're eaten up with it. I'd hoped time and distance would have helped you to see things differently. It's time you put the past behind."

Kit stood and glared at him, a mutinous expression on her face. "I know perfectly well what time it is. I think you should go now."

Sam set his half-empty bottle of Shiner on the side table and stood. He leveled an intent, fiery gaze at her. "I'm sorry you still feel that way. Unfortunately, it doesn't change what I'm about to do."

He wrapped his hand around Kit's neck and pulled her against him. She stiffened at his touch. If it were any other woman but Kit that resistance would have had him dropping his hands and stepping away. But he was determined to feel her pouty lips against his. He'd thought of nothing else since their confrontation in the parking lot at the lodge. He deliberately held her gaze before he planted a brief but crushing kiss against her angry lips, sending a shock wave through his entire body.

He released her. "Now, that's a reason to hate a Dawson." He settled his Stetson on his head, then strode to the door. "I'll save you the trouble of throwing me out."

Chapter 7

Kit hammered then pried the one-by-six inch fence board loose, gripped the sides with gloved hands, and yanked with all of her strength. Hard labor. Right now it was the only way to keep from thinking about that searing disturbing kiss. Like a red-hot branding iron, Sam's lips had made a lasting impression. Sure, he'd done it to shock her, to put her in her place, or some such macho nonsense. But instead, it'd struck a match of desire so deep it hurt. She didn't want to remember. Didn't want to think about how much she'd loved him and how much his leaving had hurt. The ache in her heart returned with such force she figured she had two choices, to stare it down or to turn and run. She decided to turn and run.

Another tug and she ripped the board clean off the post, letting it fall to the ground. She wiped her brow with the back of her hand then stepped to the other end. Standing with hands on hips, she surveyed the rotten post in front of her. She'd need the tractor to push that out. She grabbed a bottle of water from the cooler, took a long drink, then trudged back to the house. After unhooking the key from inside the kitchen door, she headed to the tractor shed. Once seated, she turned over the ignition. Nothing. She pumped the fuel line and tried again. Still nothing.

"Blast it all!"

Slapping her hat against her thigh, she jumped back down to the ground, grabbed the shovel and pickaxe, then tromped back to the post. With feet firmly planted, she swung the heavy axe up and over her shoulder and struck the ground. She repeated this process until the soil loosened.

With the palms of her hands, using the full weight of her body, she leaned into the post, pushing with all her strength. It loosened enough for her to shovel the dirt around its base. Her arms and shoulder muscles burned as she repeated this process over and over. Stopping for a breather, she leaned her weight on the shovel, then turned at the sound of horse's hooves.

Sam reined in and skimmed his eyes over Kit's slumped and dejected body. "Why aren't you using the tractor?"

Blinded by the noonday sun, Kit squinted up at him, brushed the sweat from her cheek with the back of her hand and sighed. Exhaustion oozed from every pore in her body. And from the way she'd grabbed hold of her shoulder, he could tell she was hurting.

"It wouldn't start." She was covered in sweat and grime and her plaid shirt hung partially un-tucked at her waist. Slowly, as if it pained her to do so, she removed her straw hat and swiped her brow before settling it back on her head. Lowering her eyes to the ground, she leaned the shovel against the fence.

"If this is a social call, you'll have to come back another time." She grabbed the pickaxe, swung it up and over her slender shoulder, then struck the ground near her feet.

He clenched his teeth and cursed her father for what he'd done to her. Fire burned in his gut as he watched her slam the axe over and over into the hard-packed earth.

The sound of creaking leather should have warned Kit that he had dismounted, but she kept swinging away with that damn axe like the devil himself was after her. In two strides, he reached her side and stopped the action with one hand. "Why don't you get a cool drink and sit in the shade. I'll take care of this."

Kit spun toward him, breathing hard, her chest heaving. "I've already had a drink." She lunged for the axe. "I don't need any help—"

"You're done for the day." Sam lifted the axe out of her reach, then flung it onto the ground behind him. Then, grabbing a sports drink from her cooler, he scooped her up like a sack of potatoes and headed for the shade. Her body stiffened and she slammed the palms of her hand against his chest. Glancing down at her sparkling green eyes, he gave her a look that told her she could protest all she wanted. He carried her into the shade of a nearby live oak, set her down onto her feet, then handed her the cold drink. "I don't care if you've had ten drinks. Sit down and cool off. I know when a body is ready to pass out. And, honey, you're damned close."

"What part of 'I don't want your help,' don't you understand?"

He took in her dirt-streaked face and shook his head. "Admit it. If I weren't a Dawson, you'd gladly accept my help. Wouldn't you?"

Kit closed her eyes, leaned back against the tree, and slid to the ground. "Go away, Sam."

His anger subsided at the miserable look on her face. She was beet red and seemed to be getting worse by the second. Gripped with concern, a knot formed in the pit of his stomach.

"Nope," he said, then picked her up off the ground. In seconds, he had her up and settled onto the back of his horse. The fact that she didn't fight him spoke volumes. Stepping into the stirrup, he swung up behind her, then wrapped his arms securely around her waist. Taking hold of the reins, he spurred his horse forward.

"This isn't the way back to the house." Kit squirmed in her seat. "Where are we going?"

"To the river." He had slackened his death grip around her waist but she was still hedged in-between his arms.

Minutes later, he dismounted and reached up to help Kit out of the saddle.

"Strip down and get in before you pass out."

Kit's mouth fell open. "I don't take my clothes off in front of men."

He had already yanked off his boots and was in the process of unbuttoning his shirt.

"You did yesterday."

"That was different, and you know it. I had no idea you were there."

"Come on, Kit. I've seen you in less." He gave her one of his roguish grins. The one that teased her to the core. At least that's what she used to say it did to her. He was curious to see if it still worked.

"Do you still have that little pink and yellow thing? Nothing but four patches and a couple of strings."

"It was yellow and blue. And the ties were an inch thick."

"That's not how I remember it." He peeled off his shirt and took a step toward her. For all her bravado, she was still beet red and looked hot and miserable. "Come on, Kit, get in before you pass out." She was going in the river even if he had to throw her in. "I'd be happy to help you get out of those clothes."

She stepped back. Her head darted from side-to-side.

He couldn't help it. He followed her motion from right to left. "You looking for somebody?"

"No."

"You're not thinking about yelling, are you?"

"Of course not."

If that didn't get her in the water, nothing would. Kit was a lot of things, but she'd fight tooth and nail and, on the rare occasion, even compromise, before she'd ever yell for help. So much came back to him then. He adored that scathing tone of hers. Absolutely loved the way her chin rose and her chest heaved when she got all huffy about something. How could he have forgotten? How could he have left her for so long?

"Okay, fine." She was darned hot and had actually planned to cool off in the river after her work, anyway. Squaring her shoulders, she unbuttoned the bottom button on her shirt. *Act cool. Pretend you don't give a rat's behind either way.* She unsnapped her jeans and had them down over her hips when she realized she hadn't removed her boots. Her eyes flew to his and she caught the deep twinkle in the blue-green depths.

"I'm glad you find it amusing." Humiliation spread through her as she tried to tug her jeans back up but they stuck to her hot, sweaty flesh.

"Not at all. Here, let me help?"

The humor was blatantly evident in his eyes, his expression, and his very stance. "If you laugh, I swear I'll—"

Before she knew what he'd intended, Sam brushed her off her feet and onto the ground. With one hand on her heel and the other wrapped around her calf, he tugged off one boot and then the other. Thinking he'd now help her back up, she was stunned when his strong brown hands gripped hold of her jeans and unceremoniously yanked them off her legs. Toppling backward, she landed on both elbows.

"Ouch."

"Sorry, but you're taking way too long, and I do have a business to run, you know."

"Well, don't let me stop you." She scrambled to her feet, fully revealing her powder blue panties and matching bra. She was never more thankful in her life that she was behind in the laundry, or she'd be wearing her favorite but frayed worn out underwear. Last Christmas Macy had given her the blue matching set she was now wearing and she'd never worn it until today.

His eyes roamed over her figure. She might as well have been totally naked by the way Sam was now looking at her. She stomped on the instinct to throw her hands over her chest. Instead, displaying a cool confidence, like it was part of her daily chores to strip down in front of a man, she turned and padded into the sea-green slow-moving water. Fully immersed, she reveled in the cool liquid as it flowed over her hot flesh. When she surfaced, she found Sam next to her.

Water dripped from the top of his dark brown hair over his square jaw. His lips, firm and moist, practically begged to be kissed. Raising her eyes to his, she caught her breath. She hadn't been this close to him in years. His wet lashes glistened in the dappled sunlight. For just one moment she was eighteen, wearing that little blue and yellow bikini and frolicking in this very river with her Sammy.

"Are you okay?" He swiped one brown hand across his face brushing away the excess water.

His question brought her back to the present. The concern in his eyes tugged at her heart. If he acted concerned, it'd be her undoing. But the water relaxed her. She noticed a faint scar at his hairline and before she knew what she was doing she raised her hand and gently touched the spot with her fingers.

"How did this happen?" It hadn't been there six years ago.

"I got that in a car accident."

"When?"

"A few months after I left town."

When he left town-not her. Odd how differently they saw events.

"I was wearing my seat beat or it could have been a lot worse."

"I'm glad you're all right." She gazed into his eyes for any sign of his former affection. But saw none.

He submerged completely under the water, resurfaced, and shook his dripping wet head.

"Where did you go? When you left Sugar Creek?" She asked.

"For a second his glance strayed beyond her. "Midland, Amarillo, Fort Worth, then Dallas. And a few other spots in between. Like Turkey. Have you ever been to Turkey?"

She shook her head.

"I've always wanted to go back there. Would you like to come with me, sometime?" He grinned at her. "We could take a long weekend, reminisce a little."

"I thought maybe you were seeing the world." For years after he'd left she imagined him in exotic, far away places.

"Texas is my world." Sam traced his finger along her shoulder. "Why so many questions? Don't tell me you missed me." His mouth lifted at the corners sparking a faint glint of humor in his eyes.

Kit wanted to look away from his mesmerizing gaze, but couldn't. She did have too many questions. Way too many. Like, why he left? Why he didn't come back till now? Did he fall in love? Was he dating anyone? "Why do you keep showing up?" She blurted out, hoping to change the subject.

He ran his hand through his wet hair. His gorgeous eyes, which had gone from teasing to serious, held her spellbound. She could swear he was able to see right through her. Like right now.

"To see you. To offer my help." He moved closer.

He was going to kiss her. She wanted with all of her heart to feel his lips on hers again. Sweet and tender. And one that would erase the harsh, demanding kiss from yesterday.

As if he could read her mind, he lifted his hand to her cheek. Even though it was cool and wet, tingling warmth spread from her face to her neck. She placed her hands against his firm chest while he tugged her even closer. What she wouldn't give for time to go back, for things to be the way they were before he, his father—

She jerked away, and cut through the water, splashing the blue-green river in all directions.

Scurrying up the bank, she snatched up her shirt, shoving her wet arms through the sleeves. A quick peek over her shoulder revealed Sam's bare chest, clinging boxers, and a pair of muscular thighs. Totally hot and bothered, she turned away and focused on tugging her jeans over her soaking wet flesh. Sam stood right behind her and was slipping his belt through the last loop on his jeans when she turned around.

He strode to his horse, then waited for her to join him. Suddenly tongue-tied, she couldn't say a word, and just let him help her into the saddle behind him.

This time her arms encircled his waist. Rock solid. But she already knew that. Being in his arms seared her heart like a branding iron. Then there was his tanned, rock-hard, chest as he came out of the river just now. She glanced heavenward. It took all of her willpower not to lean against his back. She sat stiffly, battling past memories of snuggling against him, her arms wrapped lovingly around his waist, content to lean against him, sheer delight in the knowledge that he was hers.

Once in the yard, Sam dismounted and waited for Kit to join him. She winced as she lifted one leg over the saddle horn, then slid off the mare, right into his arms. She stiffened as he tightened his hold.

"Thanks, but I don't need your help to get off a horse."

"That's debatable. But at least you don't look ready to pass out. Come on." He gently cupped her arm and led her through the back door.

"Sit down," he said, then walked over to the fridge and

took out a pitcher of iced tea. He filled two glasses then handed one to Kit.

He settled himself across from her, anger flaring in his eyes. "All right, where the heck is everybody? And why isn't Trip or Jake repairing that fence?"

Kit lowered her eyes. "I gave them a few days off."

"As bad as that, huh?"

"No." Her head jerked up.

"When is your next wave coming in?"

"It's hardly a wave." Her eyes met his cool stare. "Next week. Not until then."

"Are you telling me you can't afford to pay someone to help you?"

"I am paying them. They're just part time. I haven't needed anyone full time for quite a while now, since your lodge re-opened, if you must know. Besides, Macy will be back day after tomorrow and she's a great help."

"And when the Lowman sale goes through and your guests can't hunt anymore, you won't even need part time help, including Macy's. Your B&B will be closed for good."

"Thanks for the reminder but I'll cross that bridge when I get there."

"You stubborn little mule. You're on the bridge. Look, Kit, I've given you a way out. Let me have the road frontage I need and I'll give you access to all of the hunting and fishing you want. It's more than fair."

"I knew it wouldn't be long before you mentioned that. You're beginning to sound like a broken record. You're just like your old man, bargaining, wheeling and dealing. Listen to me, Sam. I'd rather lose Sage Brush a hundred times than let a Dawson have one more inch of Kendall land."

Sam raised a hand to his forehead. If she only knew how prophetic her words were. He pressed his fingers against his forehead as if warding off a headache.

"Do you hear what you just said?" He watched the color drain from her flushed cheeks. "Do you hate me that much?"

She raised stricken eyes to his then lowered them in shame. "No," she whispered.

"What makes you think I won't buy it all, once you lose it to the bank? Or, has that reality even crossed your mind?"

When she didn't answer, Sam shoved back the chair and stood. "You're running out of time, sweetheart," he said, then turned and walked out.

But not before Kit saw a small flame ignite in his eyes. Based on past experience, she knew if she wasn't careful that flame could turn into a brush fire, completely out of control.

Chapter 8

Thursday afternoon, Kit arrived at the church minutes before the bus rolled up with the kids that had gone to camp. Kit jumped down from the truck. She hadn't realized how much she'd missed Macy the past two weeks. Her energy, her voice, meant so much to her. Having her home, flitting around the house, was a link to Kit's normal world. And, buddy, right now she needed normal.

She leaned against her truck and watched the teenagers come out to hug their parents. Bags, blankets, and pillows were strewn all over the parking lot by the time the last teenager got off the bus. Kit caught Macy's eye and waved as her kid sister tumbled excitedly down the bus steps, waving back with the sparkling exuberance of a fifteen-year-old girl.

Macy had braided her long strawberry blond hair and was wearing a powder blue church camp baseball cap. Johnny Duke followed close behind and Macy stopped to speak to him. Kit watched her young sister's face. Her glowing bubbly expression displayed to anyone watching that she was definitely smitten with the boy standing in front of her. Fifteen and flirty. Her mother was really going to have her hands full.

Something tugged at her heart. She'd felt exactly the same way about Sam when she was Macy's age. Head over heels. All starry-eyed for her sweet Sammy. She knew she'd become cynical, but after what the Dawsons did, who could blame her? Her thoughts turned back to Macy as she approached. She hated the thought that someday Macy would figure it out. She, too, would entrust her heart with some good-looking, promise-you-anything guy, and then he would break it.

Macy bounded up to Kit and threw her arms around her neck. "I had the best time, ever." She linked her arms with Kit's as they headed over to the truck. "Johnny is *so* cute."

Kit smiled at Macy's enthusiasm. "So, tell me about the *mission* part of this church trip?" she couldn't resist asking.

"We had a blast. Forty-two inner-city kids attended vacation bible school. Johnny was so great with them, too. Half the little girls had a *major* crush on him. It was so sweet."

"And how about you? You got a crush on him, too?"

"Macy flashed a grin at her older sister. "Yeah. Who wouldn't? You haven't seen him up close. Oh my gosh, he has the most gorgeous brown eyes."

Macy rambled on like this all the way back to the house. Kit helped carry Macy's bags indoors then left her to get settled while she fixed them a snack. Until now, she hadn't realized how lonely she'd been without her mom or Macy around. She'd almost built up the B&B so she could afford live-in help but then McCabe's Lodge reopened and ruined that dream.

Maggie was wonderful, of course, but she had her own family and seldom stayed the night with her. Macy would live with their mom and Jeff after they returned from their honeymoon, but in the meantime was staying with Kit.

"So, where is everybody?" Macy pushed open the swinging door into the kitchen. "Why isn't Maggie here helping us get ready for the chuck wagon dinner tonight?"

Kit set the plate of sandwiches on the table then turned to get the lemonade from the fridge. "We don't have any guests this week."

"You're kidding. That's a first," Macy said as she filled two glasses with crushed ice.

Not really, but no need to say otherwise. She really couldn't blame Macy for not noticing as this was the third camp she'd been to this summer. "I thought since I had a free week, we could drive to Abilene, shop, and have lunch one day. After that, I could really use your help around here. How does that sound?"

"Cool. That works for me," Macy bit into a red plum. "Have you heard from Mom and Jeff?"

"Yeah, she emailed me yesterday to remind me to pick you up." Kit grinned.

"Oh, brother. Like I couldn't find my way home." She laughed.

Macy spun around as the brass knocker hammered against the front door. "Wonder who that is?"

Sam stood in the doorway holding a small box in his hands. He looked down at a pair of wide quizzical green eyes, and then smiled. "You must be Macy."

"Yes?"

"You don't remember me but—"

"Oh, I do remember you." She lit up. "You used to live next door. You worked for Daddy. You're old man Dawson's. I mean . . ." She looked flustered.

"That's okay, that's how I thought of him, too." He smiled and tugged on one of her braids.

"Um, please come in." Macy opened the door wider as he stepped inside.

"Thanks. Is your sister here?"

"Kit!" Macy turned and yelled. "Mr. Dawson's here to see you!"

"Call me Sam." He smiled at her.

Macy whipped back around and yelled. "Sam's here to see you!"

"Here, this is for you." Sam handed Macy the box.

She eyes lit up, then she pulled the ribbon untying the bow. When she flipped up the lid she smiled.

"Oh my gosh. Is this peanut butter taffy?"

He nodded. "Still your favorite, I hope."

"Of course." She laughed. "Thank you so much."

Kit stepped into the front hall just as Macy untied the bow.

"Look. And it's peanut butter." Macy held the box of taffy toward her sister.

"Your favorite. How nice." Kit's sarcasm totally lost on her sister.

"You're just in time for dessert," Macy told Sam while motioning him to go ahead of her into the kitchen.

Kit glanced back at Macy to see her patting a *thump-thump* over her heart with her hand. She glared at her sister, which only led Macy to perform more cupid-like antics behind Sam's back.

Ignoring Macy, Kit followed Sam into the kitchen where they all sat down for Maggie's coconut cream pie. Macy polished off her pie in record time, then excused herself.

"I have some unpacking to do so I'll see you guys later. Thanks for the taffy." This last part directed to Sam as she left the room.

Since when had her little sister become so organized? She so did not want to be left alone with Sam. Plus, it was embarrassingly obvious to her what Macy was trying to do. Catching the humorous gleam in Sam's eyes mortified her. Even he could see through Macy's attempt at matchmaking.

"She remembers," Sam said.

"She remembers nothing."

"Oh, I don't know about that." He grinned at her from across the table.

Kit inhaled deeply in an attempt to control her emotions. "She was a baby when you left."

"She was ten."

"How can you possibly remember something like that?" She scoffed.

"Because I set up the pony rides for her tenth birthday party."

"Oh yeah, I remember. My dad was . . . ill."

"He was drunk."

"Yes, he was drunk. And whose fault was that?"

Sam slowly shook his head. "Don't blame me for that one, or my father for that matter."

"Then who's to blame, huh? Who swindled him out of his land? Then financially benefited from the crude that was found on the property?"

"That was over a year later, and my father offered him a percentage of the profits."

"Peanuts compared to what should have been his."

"Your father was a fool to turn it down. He should have accepted it instead of going to court and losing even more of his money."

"He was a proud man."

"You call drinking your life away and ending up in an early grave, proud?"

Kit clamped her lips together and gazed down at her plate.

"I'm sorry, but your father's bad business decisions cannot be laid at the Dawsons' door step. There's a point in time where every man must take responsibility for his own decisions, his own actions."

"Like your father ever took responsibility for his." Suddenly, Maggie's pie tasted like cardboard.

"Let's not argue. I just came by to see Macy and give her some taffy."

"Are you sure it wasn't a bribe."

"Believe me, if I thought she had any control over your decisions, I'd have given her more than taffy." He got up as he spoke and set his plate in the sink, and then stood still as if he was listening for something.

"What?" Kit stood and pushed her chair under the table.

"It's just so quiet, that's all. This place was always a hive of activity. I have some wonderful memories here."

Kit knew Sage Brush had been like a second home to him. Suddenly, her heart ached. For what was, for what might have been, and for what she and Sam had lost. But she wasn't the one who left.

"Things will never be the way they were. I think we both know that," she said.

"I'm sorry you feel that way. But you don't speak for me, honey. Say goodbye to Macy for me. I'll see myself out."

Slowly, as if he were deep in thought, he settled his hat on his head. "There's more to this story, but frankly, you're not ready to hear it."

"What are you talking about?" Chills crept down her spine.

He didn't answer. Just strode out the back door, leaving Kit to watch him through the kitchen window until he disappeared around the corner of the house.

Chapter 9

The next morning Randy Gillian, of Gillian Electrical, handed Kit an assessment to overhaul the electrical system throughout the house.

"Jiminy Christmas, Randy. I thought Jessie James died years ago. This is twice what I'd thought it would be."

"I know, but everything's gone up. Unfortunately, we have to pass those costs over to our customers."

Kit plopped onto her desk chair and read over the assessment.

"Look, if it helps any, I'll ask my dad if he'll let you pay over a two-or three-month period."

Kit looked up at her old grade-school friend. "Honestly, I don't even know if I could swing that right now." She folded the paper and gently slapped it against the desktop. "I'll file this and hopefully I can have the work done five or six months from now." Knowing full well she probably wouldn't. She hated disappointing him. His family needed the income just like everybody else around here. The cost of overhauling the electrical system throughout the house would just have to wait.

She saw Randy to the door, then made her way upstairs. Tapping lightly on Macy's bedroom door, Kit turned the handle and peeked inside the room. "Macy, honey. It's ten o'clock. I could use your help this morning."

Macy turned her shimmering red head and squinted at Kit. "Morning." Macy stretched like a barn cat, sat up and hugged her knees to her chest. She yawned and shook her head. "So, what's up for today?"

"Basic housekeeping."

Macy groaned, fell back against the mattress, and yanked the covers over her head.

Kit laughed. "Come on. Get up, little sister. I left some pancakes under the heat light for you."

They spent the next couple of hours dusting, vacuuming, and stripping the beds for the hunters arriving on Monday. They were on the landing when the doorbell rang.

Macy raced downstairs to open the door. Johnny Duke stood in the doorway, dressed in cargo shorts and a burnt orange T-shirt, sporting the famous longhorn symbol of the University of Texas in the center. Kit entered the foyer and Macy introduced them.

Kit shook hands with the sixteen-year-old and invited him inside. Tall, with wavy brown hair and the physique of a football player, she could certainly see why Macy was smitten.

"I know I'm early, but it's my sister's birthday and I figured we could go swimming now, then you could come to her party later."

Kit frowned at Macy. "But we're were having dinner with Jake's family at the Silver Spur tonight."

Macy turned pleading eyes on Kit. "I know, but a bunch of us are going to the river to swim. And I completely forgot about Johnny's sister's party." She held the door open. "Johnny, would you like a Coke or something before we go?"

"No thanks. I was hoping we could leave now. I tired to call you earlier but you didn't answer your phone."

"Sorry, I was vacuuming."

Kit looked from one to the other. They were smiling like fools, completely unaware of her presence.

"Okay, go change and get your things while I visit with Johnny."

Macy nodded, handed Kit the dust rag, then ran upstairs.

Kit turned her attention to the confident, buff jock, who stood before her like a young bull at auction. She gave him one of her frank penetrating looks and he went from strutting to sheepish, shuffling from one foot to the other.

"So, where is this party?"

"Oh, at my house. My parents will be home if that's what you're worried about."

"What's your phone number?"

Johnny awkwardly jotted the number down and handed it to her just as Macy appeared on the landing.

She skipped down the steps and smiled up at him. "Ready?"

He nodded and Kit followed them to the door.

"Johnny, you go ahead to the car, I'll be right there," Macy said.

Kit and Macy watched Johnny walk to his Jeep Cherokee. Two of Macy's friends, Becky and Pete, were in the back seat waving. As Kit smiled and lifted her hand, Macy spun toward her. "What did you say to him?"

Kit blinked. "Nothing. I just asked for his Parent's phone number, that's all. He's new in town. It's what Mom would have done."

Macy rolled her pretty eyes. "Geez, Kit, you're going to ruin everything." She hurried down the front steps and just as she climbed into the front seat of the Jeep, she hollered, "Oh, I might spend the night with Becky, if that's okay. I'll call you."

"But you just got back," Kit yelled, but they were already leaving the driveway.

Kit slowly closed the front door and made her way to the kitchen. Last night, she'd prepared a platter of Macy's favorite mesquite chicken legs and sweet potato fries. After opening the fridge, she set the platter on the table and helped herself. She had so looked forward to Macy being at home with her. Especially this week, when there were no guests and everyone else was gone. But, her sister had her own life - her own friends, and it wasn't fair to expect Macy to fill that void.

She bit into the cold chicken and glanced around the spacious, empty kitchen. Empty of laughter. Empty of family, and of guests. In this quiet spot she was finally able to admit what she knew was true. She was lonely and for years she'd been painstakingly and methodically burying that loneliness through hard labor. Until Sam's return shook an ugly finger in her face pointing out that sad fact.

Later that afternoon, Kit stepped from the hot shower and dried off. As she rummaged through the top drawer for some underwear, she spotted the sky blue bra and panties she'd worn the other day. Fingering the lacy bra, she thought of Macy. Out on a Friday night and knowing her, having the time of her life.

Kit slipped on the powder blue underwear and then reached for a clean pair of jeans. As she did so, her eye caught the short row of dresses hanging in her closet.

After flipping through the rack, she decided on a short brown and yellow floral dress that she hadn't worn in over a year. It still fit her perfectly. Next, she pulled on her chocolate brown cowgirl boots with scalloped tops that hit mid-calf on her legs. After running her fingers through her short hair, she applied lip-gloss and mascara. Snatching up her brown leather purse, she headed out the door.

The drive into town was a short fifteen minutes. Spying a parking place, she pulled her truck between the white lines and got out. The familiar strains of Garth Books' *Friends in Low Places* bled through the walls of the Silver Spur Saloon as she approached the landmark structure. When she pushed open the door, she looked around for Jake and his family, but they hadn't arrived yet. Then she laid eyes on Sam, seated at a round table with Diana, who was dressed as if she'd just stepped off the pages of a fashion magazine. Sam, on the other hand, was dressed in a casual shirt, jeans, and boots.

For a second, he looked so much like his old self that Kit's heart skipped a beat. She may as well admit it, she missed him, with an ache she thought she'd buried long ago. Right then, he threw back his head and laughed at something Diana had said. Her heart lurched at the deep vibrant sound. It was so Sam. Right from the gut and honest.

Stop it! Turning away, she stepped up to the bar and ordered a beer. She took a swig and felt a hand on her shoulder. Thinking it was Jake and his brood, she turned around with a smile.

Sam stood there, all lean hipped and broad shouldered, smiling down at her. "Mind if I join you?"

Kit lifted her hand and gestured to the bar stool next to her. "Go ahead, I don't own the place."

Sam sat down and rested one booted foot on the brass rail near the floor. "I thought that was you, but the beer threw me. Don't tell me you quit teaching Sunday school."

She turned her pretty face toward him. "Having a beer is not a crime."

He watched as she made a deliberate action out of taking her next swig.

"You used to think so." He leaned his elbow on the bar and gazed at her profile. He still couldn't get over how short her hair was, although he could tell she'd made an attempt at styling what there was of it. He never would have thought it, but it actually suited her. Showing off her slender neck and her dainty perfect ears. And he loved the way the short copper strands brought attention to her soft temples. He had a sudden urge to kiss her right on that very sweet spot. Taking a deep, steadying breath, he asked, "You expecting someone?"

"Just Jake and his family. We're having dinner."

"Oh, I thought maybe you had a date." Sam rested his chin in his hand and watched her.

"No, but I see you do." She took a sip of the foamy malt beverage.

Sam turned and looked back to where he and Diana had been sitting earlier.

Kit swiveled in her seat, but Diana was gone.

He eyed her for some reaction but all Kit did was shrug and turn back to the bar. He thought she was doing a pretty poor job of ignoring him. He watched as she fingered her glass, knowing full well that his continued stare would begin to unnerve her. She fidgeted uncomfortably in her seat. Was she starting to unravel? *Yup.* He hated to admit it but a part of him enjoyed watching her squirm. He deserved a bit of entertainment for what she'd been putting him through.

She took a swig and stared straight ahead, while her feminine hands twisted the thick-rimmed glass between her fingers. She glanced to her left, feigning interest in everything around her, while deliberately ignoring him. He smiled to himself. It was obvious she hadn't expected to find him here. He'd seen her as soon as she'd walked through the saloon doors. From the corner of his eye, he'd watched her skid to a screeching halt when she'd noticed him sitting there with Diana. Well, she'd better get used to running into him. He wasn't going anywhere and his plans were to cut her off at the pass every chance he could.

Lucky for him, he and Diana were just finishing up a meeting. Since Kit had entered alone, he thought he'd have most of the evening to serenade her, until he found out she was expecting Jake and his family. It was probably too much to hope they'd forgotten.

Right on the heels of that thought, Jake and Elena stepped through the door. Sam turned at Jake's greeting and Kit slid off the barstool to give Elena a hug.

"Elena, you look wonderful." Kit took in Elena's black hair and sparkling brown eyes and gently patted her round belly. "Hey, baby. Your mama's glowing out here."

Elena laughed. "I think it's called sweat."

"Where's the gang? Didn't they come?"

"I left the young ones with Mom. Daniel and Jason were going to come but at the last minute had a more appealing opportunity." Elena laughed.

"I bet pretty girls were involved."

"I bet you're right? That new boy in town, Johnny Duke, invited them to a party."

"That's where Macy is tonight, too."

Jake claimed a table nearby and invited Sam to join them.

No. Please, no. Glancing from Jake to Sam to the small table for four tucked in the corner, Kit froze waiting for his replay.

"I'd love to." Sam said.

How would she ever get through dinner sitting next to Sam? Jammed against the wall. No way out. Visions of the two of them knee to knee under the table had her downing the rest of her drink in one swift gulp.

The foursome crammed around the tiny table and ordered the same thing. Bacon cheeseburgers with fries. The guys had theirs with beer and the girls had sweet tea.

"Well, aren't we a boring lot?" Jake said.

Even though Kit had inched her chair as far away from Sam's as she could, for the next half hour she became completely aware of his muscled thigh as it brushed against her leg.

"Ouch! Scoot over, friend, before I'm black and blue."
Elena laughed. "You're practically sitting in my lap."

Before Kit could say a word, Sam grabbed her chair by
the seat and slid her toward him. "Give Elena some room,
Kit. After all, she's sitting for two, you know."

Jake and Elena laughed but Kit scowled up at Sam,
seeing no humor in the situation. She was practically in
his lap.

Sam's taut, muscular thighs sparked past memories of
him behind the wheel of her Chevy, her curled up next to
him, with his free hand resting on her knees, relaxed and
comfortable because they'd belonged to each other.

Don't panic. She breathed deeply and focused on the
conversation. Football, it was something about Friday
night's scrimmage at the high school.

"The Hawks are playing the Bobcats. There'll be a good
turnout. Daniel is busting his rear end in practice. He's so
fired up."

"Like father, like son," Sam said.

"I guess." Jake chuckled.

"This is early for football, isn't it?" Kit tried her best to
focus on the conversation and not on Sam's cologne.

"Not really." Elena said. "This is one of several games
leading up to opening weekend when school starts." The
band had struck up a rowdy tune causing Elena to have
to scoot her chair closer to Kit. "All this yelling's bad for
Junior here."

"Do you need to go outside?"

"No, I'm teasing. It'll be fine."

Dinner was served and the conversation ceased as
ketchup passed from one hand to the next. The foursome
plowed into hot burgers and a mound of curly fries. Jake
grabbed a napkin and playfully wiped mustard from Elena's
chin. Kit munched on a fry and smiled. The two of them

bantered and played like teenagers. Elena sparkled up at her husband, then he leaned in for a quick kiss.

Kit glanced over at Sam and he, too, was watching them with a smile on his face. Suddenly, he looked at her, forcing Kit to lower her eyes. She reached for another fry and bit down. The band moved to a soft ballad and Elena turned her attention to Kit.

"So. How's the B&B? Jake tells me things have really slowed down lately."

Kit hesitated, then glanced at Sam. His cobalt eyes fixed on her, waiting for her response. "Jake's right." She shrugged. "But, things could be worse, I guess." She reached for a fry, hoping that was the end of the subject.

"Gosh, I sure hate to hear that. I know how difficult it was for you and your mom to get it off the ground. And now with this pokey economy." Elena pushed her plate aside. "I don't know how you do it. You've worked harder than just about anybody I know."

Kit suddenly felt awkward and desperately wanted this conversation to end.

Elena's cell phone rang from deep inside her purse.

Whew. Saved by the bell.

"Okay. We'll be right there." Elena shut off her phone and faced her husband who was talking more football with Sam. "Shug, we need to get going. Mom caught Mickey flushing her lipsticks down the toilet."

Kit hugged Elena and Jake goodbye, then grabbed her purse. As she headed toward the entrance, the band started playing Alabama's "Born Country". Sam caught up with her just as cowboys and their dates started to dance. Grabbing her arm, he spun her to his side and started the Bar-room Two-step, a version of the Texas two–step where moving sideways is allowed because of the smaller floor.

Kit tried to tug free but Sam refused to release her. Instead, he led her around the floor, and unless she wanted to cause a scene, she had no choice but to follow his lead. They executed the steps like they'd done in the past. Like Roy and Dale. In sync, one with the other. Muscle memory kicked in, and her legs and feet took over. *Triple step, triple step, step, step, turn.*

Boots scootin' and shufflin', Sam moved her backward, careful not to run her down, then sideways when the floor tightened with dancers.

Kit reveled in the movement, scooting and sliding on the wide-planked flooring with Sam's arm spanning her waist. Exhilarated, there was no way she could keep from smiling. So she didn't try. For the first time since Sam's return, she'd allowed herself to let go and enjoy the moment. Glancing up at his face, she actually smiled at him. His beautiful eyes sparkled with pleasure, crinkling at the corners.

The dance ended, and the band announced a short break, leaving them standing in the middle of the floor. As the musicians left the stage, Kit looked up at Sam. His gleaming blue eyes held a note of satisfaction as he stared at her.

"I enjoyed that. And from the looks of it, I'd say you did, too."

She was exhilarated, but she'd never admit it. "It was just a dance, Sam. Nothing more." She headed back to the table for her purse.

Sam followed close behind her. Without warning, he grabbed her around her middle, pulled her close, and whispered in her ear, "You were glowing. You loved it."

Kit tensed at his nearness and sucked in a sharp breath. Old Spice filled her senses. She fought the desire to lean back against him. She loved that fragrance. It flooded her with memories so sweet and so fine she thought her knees would buckle.

"I see you're still wearing that cheap cologne," she said, striving for a bit of composure.

"Just because something's inexpensive doesn't mean it's cheap. I've worn nothing else since you gave it to me years ago."

Allergic to most perfumes and colognes, Old Spice was one of the few fragrances that didn't give her a headache. She recalled giving him his first bottle. She'd held it out to him, then wrapped her arms around his waist. 'You'll have to wear this when we snuggle.' And boy did they ever.

She turned in his arms and darted a quick glance in his direction. By the smug expression on his face, she could tell he was remembering, too.

When he released her, she thought the tension would leave, but it didn't. What she needed was another beer. No, a real drink. She stepped up to the bar. "Whiskey, please."

Chapter 10

Sam raised an eyebrow. "Really? Gentleman Jack?" *This should be interesting.* He sat down next to Kit. "Make that two," he said to the bartender, then leaned forward and placed his elbows on the thick wooden bar. He rested his chin on his fist and stared at her. He was anxious to see how she handled her liquor. If it was anything like he'd remembered, he couldn't wait.

Kit cut her eyes in his direction. He noticed they'd taken on that intimidating quality he'd seen before. Cat-like little green slits. Which meant she'd definitely set out to prove something. Fine. He could hold his own with any man or woman.

"What are you looking at?" she asked.

"You with hard liquor. Never thought I'd see that again. Especially after the barn incident."

"You would bring that up," she hissed. "That was one time, and you know it."

"Sorry, Kitten. I know nothing of the sort. After all these years, there's no telling what you've been up to. I mean, look at you, I hardly recognize you as it is."

"Appearances can be deceiving." She shrugged. "Anyway, that happened when I was a stupid teenager."

"You weren't that young. You were sixteen. But, stupid? I'd agree to that." He raised his glass in salute.

Kit fingered her glass as a slight smile peeked from the corners of her mouth. "Boy, were you mad."

"Not as mad as your daddy when he found out," he taunted her.

"And you couldn't wait to tell him, either."

He gave her a lazy grin. "As I recall, he blistered you but good."

She rounded on him. "He did not!"

"Then what was all that hollering coming from your bedroom?"

"You were listening?" Her eyes rounded.

He knew her father hadn't touched her, but he sure as heck liked making her think he'd thought so. Donald Kendall was a weakling. That was his problem. Oh, he yelled and threatened and put up a manly front, but he was a teddy bear with his girls. The latter, one of the only good things about Kendall, as far as Sam was concerned.

"You just wanted him to. That's why you told."

"I told, so you and your boyfriend wouldn't have another opportunity to burn down the barn."

"Charlie Fletcher was not my boyfriend. That whole thing was just a stupid dare."

"Which part? The fact that your blouse was off or the empty bottle of Wild Turkey?"

Even the low light in the bar couldn't conceal the pretty shade of pink that washed over Kit's cheeks. Sam watched her finger the shot glass in her hand. She still hadn't taken the first sip.

"Trust me, it looked worse than it really was. When you stormed up the steps, I'd only had two shots."

"Two shots, and you were taking off your clothes. Good thing I arrived when I did." He raised his glass to his lips and took a sip, watching her.

Her smooth forehead creased into a frown. "We were playing strip something. You know, like strip poker, but we weren't using cards."

Sam lifted his hand to his mouth, concealing a grin at the serious expression on her face. God, she was adorable.

Kit rolled her eyes and shook her head.

"What?" Sam asked.

"I was just thinking about how you practically kicked Charlie out of the loft."

"Honey, that was minor compared to what I wanted to do to him. Especially after he mouthed off at me the way he did. I wanted to ring his scrawny neck."

"So, you took it out on me, instead." She snorted, dropped her voice an octave, and mimicked, 'Don't you have any more sense than to smoke in a barn? This place is a tinderbox. One spark, and *whoosh*!'" Kit threw her hands in the air.

"My, my what a memory." He chuckled.

"I'd hardly gotten my blouse back on before the Ranch Foreman hauled me down the steps to my father. You thought you were so tough." She rolled her sparkling eyes at him. "But you were nothing more than a twenty-three-year-old hot head."

"That's true." He nodded, then grinned. "I can still see the look on your face, though. Lower lip trembling, crocodile tears streaming down your face. You almost had me won over, too. And then I saw that empty bottle of Wild Turkey, stuffed in the hay."

Suddenly, Kit's eyes were shimmering pools of light. "I remember. You leaned toward me . . ."

"Yeah, I leaned in all right. And you reeked of whiskey." He sipped from the glass in his hand.

"I thought you were going to kiss me." She sighed.

The ready flow of sarcastic comments halted at her words. Wistful, pure longing flowed from her sparkling eyes. He was certain she wasn't aware of it. She hadn't let her guard down once since he'd returned. In the past, he'd known she'd had a crush on him. Now, he realized he should have handled her differently that night. So. She'd thought he was going to kiss her. For some odd reason he felt deeply touched. And not one to miss an opportunity, especially where she was concerned, he placed his hand under her chin, and tilted it toward him. "I'm sorry I disappointed you."

She had been quite beautiful that night, gorgeous in fact, lying in the hay wearing only jeans and a little satiny bra. His stomach tightened at the memory of her delightful curves. Until then, he'd always thought of her as the modest little cowgirl who tagged along wherever he went on the property. But the combination of seeing her shirtless, and that jock taking a drag from his cigarette, had angered the hell out of him. Then discovering the empty bottle of whiskey had released a flood of emotions that he'd never experienced in his twenty-three years. His blood still boiled at the thought. He'd already seen what alcohol was doing to her father. No way was he about to let her go down the same path. Not if he could help it. In that moment, he realized how much he really cared for her. But, truth be known, discovering her with that arrogant jerk was what had angered him most of all.

Kit pulled her chin from his hand breaking the spell. It was her turn to shrug. "No biggie."

He took her hand in his, thankful when she didn't resist. "Kit, I was a young hothead, but you know I was right."

She sighed. "Of course, you were right. When I think of the horses, the danger, I still get sick about it." She ran her fingers behind her ear. "When I realized what could have happened, I cried for days. And from that moment on, I've never had another drop of whiskey." She looked over at him, all wide-eyed and appealing. As if she was trying to convince him of that fact.

He eyed the glass wrapped tightly in her fingers. "Until now."

She shrugged.

"People change, Sam.

"Yes, they do." He lifted his glass in salute. "To change." He tossed it back, then waited for Kit to do the same.

He watched Kit turn from him to stare at the shot glass. She was sure taking her time about it.

"Building up the nerve?"

That did it. Kit picked up the glass and tossed the fiery liquid down her throat. Stifling a cough, she squeezed her eyes shut, then grimaced.

I knew it. She hates the stuff. He watched her whole body shiver before she set the glass onto the counter.

"Pour me another," she said. The bartender tipped the bottle, splashing amber liquid into her glass.

Sam motioned for him to leave the bottle.

This time Kit didn't stop to think. She downed the whiskey and slammed the glass back down on the bar. So, if two drinks was all it took for her to shed her clothes, then what would three or four have her doing? Her eyes should at least be glazing over by now. But amazingly, they weren't. So he did what any respectable cowboy would do under the circumstances. He poured her another drink. He was curious to see how far she'd take this charade.

Setting the bottle down, he waited for the entertainment to begin.

Fifteen minutes later, Kit lifted her glass. "To Mr. Jack."

"Hear, hear." Sam raised his and they chinked their glasses together. Then he watched Kit down the fifth glass of the golden liquid. He shook his head. Amazed at her fortitude, he smiled. Apparently, she had more iron lining her stomach than he'd realized. Over the next half hour, he'd watched Kit go from stiff-necked to down right sultry.

He looked at his watch. Ten-thirty p.m. Apparently, she didn't know when to stop. Another sign of a rookie.

"Too early to be this drunk. I think you've had enough." Sam took a large bill from his wallet and slapped it on the bar just as the band struck up "All My Ex's Live in Texas".

"Oh, I love this song." With a sudden jerk, Kit turned to him. "Let's dance," she said, and grabbed his arm.

Whiskey sloshed everywhere. With a careful motion, he placed his glass on the counter, grabbed a napkin, and wiped the excess whiskey off his hand.

"I have a better suggestion. Let me take you home."

"Home? There's nothin' there. Nobody's there. Why do you want to go there? I wanna dance." Kit slid off the barstool and tugged on his arms.

He stood up and placed his hands on her shoulders to steady her. "This party's over."

"Honey." Kit leaned into him, pressing her lovely slender self against his chest. "This party's just beginning," she slurred.

This, he hadn't prepared for. A delicate pink flush covered her skin. Her face, neck, and shoulders glowed under the soft bar lights. Her velvet flesh pressed into his chest. He groaned, encircled her with his arms and lowered his head.

Kit was gazing up at him, asking, no, begging to be kissed and he was more than happy to oblige. Warm breath that held a hint of whiskey filled his senses. Green eyes sparkled with such sweet abandon, that it was almost his undoing. But before his lips could claim hers, Kit slipped from his arms. He tried to grab her but missed when two guys pushed up to the bar, separating them. He maneuvered his way through the throng of bodies and just as he was about to reach her a couple stepped into his path.

Enough of being a gentleman. He clamped his jaw shut and shouldered his way through the crowd just in time to see her climb up onto the bar.

Oh no.

Before he could stop her, Kit started to stomp across the dark wooden surface. Keeping time to the music with her brown boots, she raised her arms and twirled to the rowdy drinking song blaring through the saloon. The bar crowd hooted and howled, clapped and sang along, their energy empowering her to twirl and shimmy. And when she started singing at the top of her lungs, Sam lifted his hand to his forehead.

It usually took a hell of a lot to shock him, but this foot stomping, twirling, cowgirl rendered him speechless. As he watched her a smile tugged at the corners of his mouth. She was tipsy, all right. And she was amazing. He'd never seen her like this. This was total, joyful abandon.

He folded his arms across his chest surrounded by the throng of rowdy cowboys and watched her. She was almost on top of him when he noticed he could see her powder blue panties. All silk and lace. And if he could see, so could every other heathen standing at this damn bar. Anger flared in his gut.

He waited until Kit was right in front of him. Then he reached up, grabbed hold of her gyrating hips, and lifted her off the bar. He threw her over his shoulder and pressed his way through the crowd. Brown cowgirl boots kicked madly, cutting through the smoke-filled room. The thud of her puny fists pummeling his back as he carried her through the crowded bar only made him more determined to get her safely outside.

"Go ahead and give me hell." He flung the words over his shoulder. "I'm not putting you down until I get to my truck." With his free hand, he pulled the keys from his pocket. Unlocking the door was a bit difficult but he finally managed. After yanking the door open, he plopped her onto the passenger seat.

Satisfied she was still in one piece, he shut the door. In seconds, he was seated next to her behind the wheel. He turned to her and his heart all but stopped. Kit had turned green.

"I don't feel so good." She moaned and leaned back against the new leather upholstery.

"Oh no. Not in my new truck, you don't."

Sam shot out of his seat and circled around the front of the vehicle faster than he could spit. He yanked open the door just as Kit heaved. Lightning couldn't have been any faster. He grabbed her under her arms and pulled her out just as she threw up. Her rear end was still somewhat seated in the truck and she was hanging out of the open door like a rag doll. Sam supported her by the shoulders and held her forehead until she was finished. When she sat up, her face was pale and thankfully the only green he could see was in her eyes.

He took one look at the inside of his truck, thanked God, then grabbed a half-used bottle of water from under the seat and handed it to Kit.

"Here, swish and spit."

Like an obedient child, Kit did as she was told. When she was done, she laid back against the seat. The pathetic look on her face reminded him of a stray puppy. He tried not to smile, but his lips seemed to have a will of their own and lifted anyway. "You okay?"

Kit swallowed and shook her head.

"So, you're not okay."

"I need to lie down." She then sprawled across the center armrest.

Sam gently lifted Kit off the hard console and settled her back in the passenger seat. Clicking the seat belt in place, he pressed his thumb against the electronic seat button. By the time the seat was all the way back, she had passed out.

Twenty minutes later, Sam held Kit against his chest while he rummaged through her purse for the key, wishing like heck he'd thought to retrieve it while they were still in the truck. He finally felt it in the bottom of her purse, pulled it out, and unlocked the door.

The house was dark as he entered. He called for Macy, but there was no answer. After he carried Kit up the stairs to her bedroom, he switched on the bedside lamp, then laid her on her bed. He pulled off her boots, then tucked her in. Stuffing his hands in his pockets, he stood over her for a moment before going downstairs. In minutes he was back with a pitcher of water and a glass. He set it on the bedside table, then hauled Kit to a sitting position. She moaned and opened her eyes.

"Kit. Wake up. You have to drink water. You're going to have one heck of a headache in the morning as it is, but this should help."

"Go away." She moaned. "Let me sleep." She pushed on his chest.

"I didn't know you were such a whiney baby."

Kit tried to give him her evil eye but failed miserably. "That's more like it. Now drink this and I'll let you go back to sleep."

She gulped as much water as she could before finally turning her head away. "I'm gonna throw up," she wailed.

"No more. You're done." He laid her back against the pillow, wondering how she could be this sick after only six or seven shots. As he pulled the sheet upward, Kit reached up and took hold of his shirt. He gazed down at her and groaned. It was all he could do not to take her in his arms. She was completely vulnerable. He knew if he'd wanted to, he could get away with just about anything right now. She was more than asking for it. Her eyes glistened like emeralds, set off by wisps of shiny red bangs and creamy skin. Pleading. Desiring. Beckoning. She was like an unlocked vault where any thief could waltz right in and take what he wanted. Dear Lord, he wished to God she wasn't drunk.

In that moment, his desire for her nearly overwhelmed him. Drawing on every ounce of his strength, he placed his hands over hers and pulled them off his shirt. Holding her hands in his, he looked down at her.

"Sammy?"

Raw ache filled him.

"Yes, honey."

"You left me." She choked back a sob. "You left me." A large tear escaped and coursed down her cheek.

Kit stared up at him. Her tearful green eyes held a hurt so real and raw he could almost touch it.

That was all the excuse he needed. He gathered her in his arms and held her close, knowing she'd most likely hate herself in the morning for being so vulnerable with him.

Kit jabbed weakly against his arm with her fist. "I hate you." Even though the words were muffled against his chest, he felt the full impact cutting straight to his heart.

"I know."

"You left me." She whimpered and repeated herself and over and over until he thought his heart would break. Sometime later, she had fallen asleep in his arms. Unable to take his eyes off her, he watched her breathe, and held her until his arm muscles burned from the strain. Settling her against her pillow, he stood up, stretched the ache from his arms, then crashed on the love seat. He should probably leave but he couldn't. He'd left her once, but never again.

Chapter 11

Kit slowly opened her eyes and felt something like needles shoot through her forehead. She moaned. Her stomach rocked, and she had to pee. The pounding in her head grew and screamed for medication. The covers felt like dead weight. She pushed them off her, then dangled her legs over the side. She noticed she was still in her dress. Standing proved to be more difficult than she'd thought. Dizzy and disoriented, her head felt like a gold fish bowl on a stick. The floor moved beneath her feet. After stopping twice, she finally made it to the bathroom. She took a couple of pain pills, then plopped down on the toilet.

Sixty seconds later, she stumbled back into her bedroom. She was at the foot of her bed when she saw him. Sprawled out on her loveseat eyeing her from underneath his hat. Kit froze.

"Don't worry. I didn't hear a thing." Sam grinned.

She sucked in her breath. "What are you—?" She squeezed her eyes shut against the head-splitting pain shooting through her temples and grabbed the bed post for support. "Doing in my bedroom?" she finished.

As soon as the words were out of her mouth, she remembered. Well, sort of remembered. To say last night was hazy was putting it mildly. A complete blur was more like it.

"Relax, kitten. We're both fully clothed and I'm still on the couch." He pushed his way to a sitting position and adjusted his hat farther back on his head. His smile sent shivers down her spine. "You look like you could do with some coffee," he said as he stood to his six-foot, two-inch height.

"What happened last night? Oh, wait. I remember." She groaned and dropped her face in her hands. "I can't believe I did that. I never do anything like that."

She glanced at Sam, his expression serious. "I'm not like my father. At least not in that respect."

He towered above her. Was he taller than normal, or was she shrinking? Her legs buckled and in two short strides Sam grabbed her around her waist.

"Here, lie back down." He helped her back to her bed. "I figured as much." His mouth quirked at the corners. "But, just the same, I'm glad to hear you admit it. I'll go make coffee."

Kit relaxed against the pillows. The chink of pottery against wood and stainless steel echoed up the stairs.

Ten minutes later, Sam walked through her doorway with a tray of coffee, Maggie's biscuits and homemade strawberry jam.

When he entered the room, Kit tried to get up.

"Nope. You just stay right there. A few crumbs on your sheets aren't going to hurt anything."

"I'm not worried about crumbs."

"Then what?" He eyed her with that delicious gleam. One she'd seen many times in the past. The one that always made her heart lurch and her breath catch.

"Maggie and Macy, that's what."

"It's early, kitten. Besides, they're not here. I've already checked."

"And what is this 'kitten' nonsense?" Sam turn his attention from her to a warm biscuit. He lifted a butter knife and liberally spread jam over the white fluff and handed it to her.

"Sorry. Old habits die hard. Here. Eat. And drink your coffee before it gets cold."

Gruffness had come over him. She didn't blame him. He couldn't have gotten much sleep on her love seat. He was sporting a morning shadow giving him an utterly, appealing, roguish look.

"Have you ever thought about growing a beard?" She nibbled at her biscuit.

He nodded. "I actually had one until I got back here. I'd been in Montana for six weeks touring hunting and fishing camps. They're owned by a friend of mine. He takes guests out for a week or two at a time. Depending on the season, they fly fish and hunt elk. They pack everything on mules and they ride horses into the wilderness. It's marvelous. No cell coverage, but all the amenities of a five-star resort. Tents, the size of rooms, are set up for their guests. They bring a chef and he not only cooks what they catch, but serves it with the most amazing side dishes." He lifted his fingers to his lips and kissed them. Then bit into the biscuit he fixed for himself.

"Better than Maggie's cooking?" she couldn't resist asking.

His eyes flew to hers. "You know better than that." His reprimand held a subtle twinkle. "Seriously, though, I do think there's room for both. People want variety. They want hearty home cooked and five-star cuisine, in all of its glory.

"Is that your plan? To give both?" She realized she was holding her breath for his answer. If she could discover his plans, it would shed some light on what she was really up against. Knowing full well, at this very moment, she would never be able to compete. Not with what he had just described.

He brushed a crumb from his shirt and then downed the rest of his coffee. "That's exactly the plan." He stood. "Finished?"

She gazed up at his ruggedly handsome features. Feeling suddenly lost, she nodded then watched him stack the mugs and plates. Her gaze locked on to his strong hands, bronzed from the Texas sun, as they gripped the sides of the tray with the ease of a man not at all averse to the common goings on of everyday life. "I'll see you later," he said.

His smile still sent her heart into overdrive.

Damn him.

Wednesday morning, Kit sat in her office, staring down at the tax bill in her hands. A wave of nausea gripped her in the pit of her stomach. Fifteen thousand. May as well be fifty. Placing her elbows on the desk, she lowered her head in her hands. Here was a giant she'd never be able to handle. Defeat, full and sudden, crushed her like a collapse in a gold mine. She pushed away from the desk. She'd have to go see Mr. Brown at the bank.

An hour later, she sat across from him in his office.

"Kit, you know I'd help you if I could, but another extension on your loan is out of the question." He placed his elbows on the desk and leaned toward her, his gray eyes serious. "They're breathing down my neck as it is. I'd lose my job if I made such a decision. You're now two and a half months delinquent on your payments. The main office is chomping at the bit to get a hold of your place. They want their money."

"Don't they understand this land has been in my family for generations?" Kit's eyes filled with tears. "I'm doing everything I know to do."

"Everything but accept Dawson's offer."

Kit tensed. "How do you know about that?"

"Don't look so surprised. He's been in here three times to talk with me about it."

"You're in cahoots with him?"

"You know better than that."

She did. Ted Brown was her father's friend and that was the only reason he was going the extra mile with her now. But, it didn't help matters any. Trapped. That's what she was. Trapped, like a rabbit in a deep hole. With her only option to sit huddled in the bottom waiting for either a rescuer or a predator. Somehow she knew it would be the latter.

Shoulders slumped, she stood. "I'll think of something, Mr. Brown."

"I hope so."

She could see the sadness in his eyes. Kit knew he'd done all he could, considering the circumstances. With the recent acquisition by First Texas Bank and Trust with Sugar Creek Bank, she knew this wasn't a mom and pop bank anymore."

"Kit?"

"Yes?"

"I hope I'm not speaking out of turn, but I've known your family for many years." He hesitated.

"Go on," she said, somewhat intrigued.

"I was thinking about that offer your mother had a while back. And I know it's not ideal, but I wish you'd reconsider it. I know the buyer is still interested. You'd have enough for a brand new start. In this economy, there are a lot of small ranches for sale. I'm sure you could find a good buy. Anyway, just something to think about."

They shook hands and Kit walked outside into the sunshine, squinting against the glare after being in the low light of Brown's office. That was two people who'd suggested she sell her homestead. First Maggie and now Mr. Brown. She sighed. Maybe as a last resort, if things got really bad, she'd have to. But, not until then. She stopped in her tracks. The mere fact that she'd even contemplate such an action grieved her.

Adjusting her purse strap on her shoulder she turned right and walked down the pavement toward her truck. Heat rose from the sidewalk like steam from a boiling kettle. She passed one of the new restaurants in town and stopped. The Fat Canary was a new top-end eatery that everyone had been raving about.

A 'Help Wanted' sign was just being placed in the window. The part-time position could be perfect for her. Heaven knew she needed the extra money and depending on the hours, it just might work. Plus, it wasn't like she had hordes of people visiting. On impulse, Kit pushed open the door and went inside.

"Table for one?" The pretty young brunette cocked her head to the side.

"Ah, no. I'm actually here about the 'Help Wanted' sign."

"Oh, sure. Let me get Henry. Wait here."

Kit watched the girl glide away. She was dressed in a tight-fitting black dress Kit could have sworn she'd been poured into. Scrunching up her nose, she looked around the restaurant. That couldn't be the standard uniform, could it? How could she possibly wear such a thing?

Two days later, Kit stared wide-eyed at her reflection in the full-length bedroom mirror. Green eyes peeked back at her image from under her red bangs, like saucers. The shocked squeak that escaped her lips sounded a lot like her mother's the night Kit had come downstairs for her high school junior prom, dressed in that green skimpy low-cut taffeta scrap of material she'd had the nerve to call a dress. Her mother had sent her right back upstairs to put on something more 'seemly' for a girl her age.

Kit groaned. She so could not wear this in public. She had told Henry, the manager of the restaurant, that very thing, after he'd interviewed her. But he'd quickly informed her, 'No little black dress, then no job. I certainly understand if you're not comfortable wearing it, but that's the look the owner wants. It's up to you, of course, but I think you'd be great, especially with your B&B experience. So what do you say? I need someone right away.'

Out of desperation she'd said yes. But now, standing in front of the mirror with an embarrassingly generous amount of white flesh on display, she was beginning to have second thoughts. Her hands crept up to touch her exposed skin above the low-cut fabric of the dress. She started her evening shift in one hour. Should she call Henry and back out? Then she thought of the tax bill and reason flew the coop like chickens from a fox.

Still gazing at her reflection, she hardly recognized herself with all of that makeup. Another part of the dress code, according the Rebecca, the assistant manager.

Nothing for it. It had to be done. After all, this was a life or death situation as far as she was concerned. Her future and her B&B were at stake. Kit squared her shoulders, wrapped an oversized sweater tightly around her body, then headed out the door.

Parking on the side street near the restaurant, Kit got out of her truck and locked it. She scanned the surrounding area, thankful no one she knew was in sight. Quickly, she made her way around the block and into the restaurant without seeing anyone.

Heck, what did it matter? Someone she knew would undoubtedly show up to eat and then what? *Buck up, girl.* There was a time you'd have killed to dress like this.

Kit made her way to the back and hung her sweater on a shiny stainless steel hook.

A slender blond, with shoulder-length hair, approached her. For someone who sported such a svelte figure and stylish glamour, her smile said sweet and friendly.

"Hi, I'm Pam. You're Kit, right?"

Kit smiled back. "That's me."

"Here's your apron. Henry likes these half jobs. Shows off our dresses."

Pam's eyes held a twinkle Kit found contagious.

"Yes, and a few other things." Kit laughed.

"Hey wait." Pam paused and eyed Kit curiously. "I know you."

"You do?"

"Yeah. You're the girl who danced on the bar the other night."

Kit's mouth went dry. "You saw that?"

"I sure did. Along with just about everyone else in town." Pam laughed. "You're famous."

Kit tied the apron around her waist. "About the bar thing. That's not really me."

Pam eyed Kit up and down and grinned. "Honey, the way you look in that dress, nobody's gonna believe that."

Kit blinked rapidly. Time to change the subject. "Henry told me you and Rebecca weren't from around here. How in the world did you end up in Sugar Creek?"

"Rebecca and I worked at their sister restaurant in Dallas and when this one opened we decided to leave city life for a while. I really like it here. Henry says to expect more of this sort of thing once the resort takes off. I'm from Fort Worth, by the way."

"I know Fort Worth. All my boots are M.L.Leddys. Custom," Kit said.

"Mine, too. Gabe's the best, isn't he? And such a cutie." Pam smiled.

Kit followed Pam to the dining room where Pam filled her in on the protocol and showed Kit her tables.

Rebecca unlocked the front door and several older couples filed in for an early dinner, beating the rush.

Kit was surprised that she didn't know anyone who came in to dine then realized they must all be from the resort. She had to confess to being surprised at the caliber of people that she'd waited on. They were friendly and displayed patience and understanding that this was her first day on the job.

By the fourth table, Kit had the specials down pat and rattled them off with style and finesse. The evening flew by and before she realized it, the place was closed and she was hanging up her apron.

"You did great tonight," Pam said. "Saturdays are killers most of the time. Especially in a town where there's not many options."

"Speaking of killers, I think my feet are dead." Kit pointed to her high heels. "How do you wear these things?"

"You'll get used to them." Pam laughed. "When are you working again?"

"Tomorrow night."

"Gosh, Saturday and Sunday night. Henry has a lot of confidence to start a newbie on both of those nights."

"Probably, a case of sink or swim." Kit laughed. "Are you working tomorrow?"

"Oh yeah."

"Great, then I'll see you tomorrow." Kit pulled on her sweater and stepped out on the sidewalk. She hurried to her truck and unlocked the door, then pulled out her cell phone to call Macy. When she didn't answer, Kit left her a message that she was on her way home.

After working all day on the ranch, then waiting tables at night, Kit had to practically drag herself up the back steps.

She pushed open the back door and was hit with the sweet aroma of baked cookies. Macy and Johnny were sliding warm chocolaty things off the baking sheet onto a cooling rack.

Macy's eyes widened as Kit entered the kitchen. Perplexed at her sister's reaction, Kit raised a brow at her sister. Macy's jaw then dropped a good two inches before Kit realized why. She glanced down, and to her horror, the sweater had flopped open revealing parts of her that should have remained hidden, especially from the sixteen-year-old Johnny, whose jaw had joined Macy's on the floor.

Kit felt her face flush as she snatched the sweater together.

"What the heck are you wearing? Let me see that." Macy, now bubbling with excitement, ran over to her and pealed the sweater from Kit's fingers, which had turned white from clutching the fabric tightly against her chest.

"Macy, for gosh sakes." She snatched the sweater back frantic that Macy would completely disrobe her. "It's my uniform."

"What uniform?"

"I work at that new fancy restaurant in town. The Fat Canary." Then with clenched teeth, she added in a low voice. "And if you'd been home for the past couple of days instead of out playing, you'd have know about it."

Macy eyes glistened like she'd just discovered gold. "When can I sign up?"

"Don't be silly. You have to be twenty-one to work there," she said, trying to sound calm. "Johnny, pick your jaw up off the floor. You'll catch a fly with your mouth open like that."

"Yes, ma'am." He gave Macy a sly smile that clearly said he had no idea Macy had a *sister like that*.

"Johnny, I think you'd better get going," Macy said. "I'll see you tomorrow."

Summarily dismissed, Johnny let himself out the back door.

"Okay. He's gone. Now take off that sweater." Macy grabbed the fabric and started to peel it off Kit's shoulders.

Kit rolled her eyes. "Okay, fine." Then she slipped off the long-sleeved cover-up.

"Wow. You look fantastic."

Kit pursed her lips together.

"I mean it, Kit. You're beautiful. And you're even wearing makeup."

An honest look, something near big-sister adoration, flowed from Macy's eyes. Touched, Kit smiled. She knew Macy meant it as a compliment but didn't want her to think this was normal for her.

"Thank you, but truthfully, I'm really uncomfortable in this getup."

"Why? That's so silly. Have you looked in the mirror?"

"Unfortunately, yes. And I look ridiculous. This may be you, but it's not me. Comfortable cotton dresses are all I've ever worn, and that's when I used to wear dresses."

"Has Sam seen you in that?"

"Heck no."

Macy just shook her head. "Since when did you start acting like some old maid?" She slid another cookie onto the cooling rack.

Crushed, Kit turned away, not wanting Macy to see how much her comment had hurt her. "I'm going to bed," she said over her shoulder and then made her way upstairs. What Macy failed to recognize was that she had no use for men. So, why in the world would she deliberately dress to attract them? But, if she had no use for men, then why did Macy's 'old maid' comment hurt so much?

Chapter 12

Sunday night, Sam had just parked and was walking up the alley when he saw Kit slip out the back door of the restaurant. The light from the streetlamp poured over Kit's smooth white flesh, reminding him of that day at the river. He stopped in his tracks. What was she doing here? And in that particular dress?

She hadn't noticed him so he took the moment to enjoy the vision. If he hadn't already known who she was, he'd swear she was a sexy lingerie model. She slipped off her heels and crossed one leg over the other - the action hiked her skirt right up to the top of her thighs. With her short hair tucked behind her ears, her perfectly made up face and those creamy long legs, she was a knockout. In that moment she was pure magic. A lovely damsel-in-distress perched on the top step with a sweet pained expression on her delicate features. His gut did a somersault.

She bit her lower lip with even white teeth and her forehead creased in something between pain and ecstasy as she continued to massage her feet. When she closed her eyes and moaned, his gut knotted into a tight ball. Her full, slightly parted lips reminded him of fresh-picked strawberries.

"You look like you could use a little help."

Kit's eyes flew open and her head snapped up. Not only did her serenity leave, but also her hands from her feet. As he slowly approached, her knees snapped together in a rigid pose. She quickly glanced over her shoulder at the back door of the restaurant. It amused him to think she'd considered a run for it. In seconds, she went from siren to schoolgirl, her wide sparkling green eyes staring up at him. Surely she wasn't turning red. Any moment now and her skin would match her hair. He stifled a grin. This was the Kit he remembered. She hadn't changed. Not one little bit. For all the bravado of the past few weeks, she was still the girl next door. The girl he'd left behind.

"What are you doing here?" She gasped.

I was about to ask you the same question. He shrugged. "Just passing by."

"Sure you were."

He watched the lovely rise and fall of her breasts, much of which were not covered by . . . anything. Her hands groped to cover her exposed flesh and the tightness in his gut got tighter.

"You always seem to think the worst of me," he said.

"Are you spying on me?"

"Like that, for example." Sam grabbed his lower lip between his teeth and watched Kit squirm under his scrutiny. He couldn't help but enjoy himself at her expense. After all, she had been the source of constant turmoil to his business, not to mention his own peace of mind. The least she could do was suffer a bit of embarrassment—the reason her formerly creamy skin was now the exact color of her hair. He smiled at her. A slow deliberate smile. He couldn't help it.

Suddenly unable to move or to speak, she sat frozen before him. She placed one hand on the hem of her skirt and tugged. Her attempts to pull her dress down over her thighs proved unsuccessful. He took note of how her pretty little toes curled up. How one foot slid over the other in complete agitation. She was completely unnerved. Her eyes lifted. He caught the slightest hint of pleading in their green depths and found it difficult to resist. The unexpected tug on his own heart didn't surprise him. He'd always had a soft spot for those emerald eyes of hers.

All right. You've had your fun. He admonished himself.

Her tongue traveled over her red lips. Suddenly, he wanted to kiss those lips. To cup her face in his hands, kiss away her wounds, and tell her not to worry. The sudden urge to make her feel safe pulsed through his veins. Should he ignore her stubborn pride, her unfair accusations? Yes, he should. He was not his father. He was a gentleman. A cowboy. A Texan.

Truth be known, it killed him to know that she'd rather take a waitressing job before she'd work in his hotel or sell a scrawny piece of dry ground to him.

He got down on his haunches in front of her. Her wide, appealing eyes glowed with embarrassment. Her breaths quickened and he watched her exposed flesh rise and fall with each breath she took.

Sam took hold of one of her feet and heard her sharp inhale. Gently, he squeezed and rubbed his hands over her foot before administering aid to the other one.

"Oh, yeah. Right there."

A sweet sigh escaped her lips. He was certain if she could have avoided it, she would never have let him know how good his actions had made her feel. Her feet had to be killing her. When he finished he gently slipped her feet back into her shoes. "You should wear flat ones."

Then he stayed right where he was and looked at her, waiting for some response. She seemed reluctant, cautious, and could barely look him in the eye. But his continued stare gave her no choice but to acknowledge him. She ran her tongue over her lips, an action he thoroughly enjoyed watching.

"I can't. House rules."

"I know the owner. Maybe the rules can be changed." She raised her eyes to his and he drank in her loveliness. She'd covered her freckles with makeup and he had this sudden urge to wipe it off so he could see them. Bathed in the light from the streetlamp, she was the most kissable creature he'd seen all day. Kit lowered her gaze and her long lashes swept across her cheeks like tiny fans.

She drew in a slow breath, licked her lips, then swallowed. "Thank you." She ran her finger behind her ear. "I have to go back in. I've been out here too long. Pam's probably wanting to murder me by now."

Her smile was tremulous and sweet. His heartbeat quickened. He stood then and held out his hands to her. She placed hers in his and he helped her to her feet. She gazed up at him and he almost lost his breath. She was beautiful. He hadn't intended to, but he leaned forward and kissed her. She tasted like coconut cream pie. One sweet quick taste, and regret filled his soul. He'd give just about anything to kiss her senseless. But he reined in his emotions. He wasn't some uncontrolled spirited stallion in the wild. Yes, he wanted more. He wanted her. But there was too much excess baggage between them. Too many painful memories he knew she needed to get over. And, God help him, he had no idea how to help her get there.

Kit tried to make sense of Sam's attention. She couldn't help but feel that he was up to something as far as she was concerned. She hated that he'd witnessed her in such a getup. Glancing down, her display of flesh made her cringe. That he'd found her in such skimpy attire was more than she could stand. She felt her skin flush again with embarrassment. But for just a moment she let her mind drift back to the pleasant feel of his hands on her sore feet. The way his attentive eyes seemed to look right into her very soul. She'd always found it difficult to hide her thoughts from him, especially when he looked at her with those penetrating blue eyes of his.

"Hey, what kept you? You have a group at table four. I've already taken them water," Rebecca said.

"Oh, gosh. I'm sorry. I'll get right on it." Kit slipped the order tablet from her apron pocket and hurried into the dining room. She skidded to a halt when she saw who was seated at her table. Sam and Diana and two other couples. Her heart raced and her stomach felt like it was filled with butterflies, with their tiny wings beating against her ribs in a flurry to get out. Taking a deep breath to settle her nerves, she pasted on her best smile and approached the table.

"Good evening. I'm Kit and I'll be your server this tonight."

"What happened to the other girl?" Diana asked, somewhat peevishly.

"She was just helping me out. I was on break." Her eyes flew to Sam's face before she refocused on the group. "Have you dined with us before?"

Diana let out a low chuckle and then smirked at the others at her table. She then raised an eyebrow at Sam that only accentuated her smirk making Kit feel like she had missed the punch line of a joke.

"Yes we have, Kit." Sam spoke with a pleasant tone, flashing Kit one of his brilliant smiles.

"Great." Her hands shook as she took their drink order. After she went over the specials, she made her way to the bar where Louie, the bartender, filled the drink order.

After Kit served them their drinks, she went to the kitchen and turned in their dinner order, then served her next table.

It was a packed house and hustling back and forth between tables and the kitchen took its toll on her feet. She limped to the ladies' room clenching her teeth against the pain from the blister that had formed on her right heel. Closing the lid on the toilet, she sat down and pulled a small wad of tissue off the roll, then gently placed it over her heel before sliding her foot back in the shoe.

Kit jumped at the sudden pounding on the door. "Just a minute!"

"Hurry it up, gorgeous. You've got two tables that are ready for their tickets," Henry said.

"I know. I know. If I could just walk," she mumbled.

The paper held in place while she took care of Table Six but began to slip, exposing raw flesh to the leather heel, just as she got to Sam's table. Limping forward she took his credit card, turned and then hobbled to the computer to make the payment. She bent down to slide the tissue back in place but it had slipped out on the floor somewhere. "Great." Walking back to the table was painful and by the time she got there sweat had broken out on her upper lip.

Sam looked up at her after signing the ticket. "You okay?"

Her gaze locked with his. "Blister."

"Well, it's no wonder," Diana chimed in. "Have you ever even worn heels before?"

Kit clamped her teeth together more from Diana's comment than her heel pain. But, before she could respond, Diana had turned her attention to the other guests at the table as they all stood to leave.

Kit wished them goodnight and walked away, trying her best not to limp.

Chapter 13

Monday morning brought another scorcher. The incessant heat and lack of rain made the day more miserable than the one before. After applying antibiotic cream and a fresh Band-aid to her blister, Kit slipped on her house slippers and went downstairs.

Sitting at her desk, hot coffee in one hand and the tax bill in the other, she stared at the amount on the paper. Maybe if she concentrated hard enough the numbers would change. She lowered her head to her hands and felt the familiar, almost daily, knot form in the pit of her stomach. She'd have to let Jake go. If someone had told her a year ago that she'd have to let three guides go over the course of two months, she wouldn't have believed them. Her fingers shook as she picked up the office phone and dialed his number. When he didn't answer she left a message for him to come by. She'd tell him today after he came back from getting the tents and other supplies set up for the hunting party that was to arrive later that afternoon.

Kit slid the bill in the desk cubby and went into the kitchen, where she found Macy ladling up breakfast.

"Mmm, something smells good."

"Peach muffins, scrambled eggs, and bacon." Macy set the plates on the table and sat down.

"Peach muffins. I'm impressed, little sister."

"Don't be. There're from a box." Macy laughed.

After breakfast, Kit and Macy spent the next several hours getting ready for their guests.

"How come Maggie's not here to help?" Macy asked as she struggled with an unruly pillow and its case.

"Pete's home for a short stint before he goes to summer school and I wanted her to have some time with him."

"Oh, I thought it might be because we don't seem to have many guests." Macy shot Kit a sly glance that spoke volumes.

Kit felt a slight flush to her already hot cheeks and glanced back at Macy. "Here, let me have that," she said as she took the half stuffed pillowcase from her sister. "So, you've noticed," she added as she crammed the pillow in place.

"Yeah, I've noticed. What's the deal?"

"The deal, little sis, is McCabe's Resort Lodge. They're putting a pretty little pinch on my business."

In unison, they straightened the sheets and pulled up the bedspread.

"I'll say. How long has this been going on?"

"For a good while, but it wasn't that bad until they finished the golf course. Since then, business has steadily gone downhill."

"Is that why you took the restaurant job?"

Kit nodded.

"Gosh, Kit. I'm really sorry." Macy walked around the foot of the bed and gave Kit a hug. "And, I'm sorry I haven't been more help to you."

"You're a great help, when you're not flirting with Johnny Duke." She grinned and then tossed the pillow on the bed.

"Anybody here?"

Kit and Macy turned their heads toward the door. "Oh, that's Jake. Finish up, okay. I need to talk to him."

Kit left the bedroom and saw Jake standing at the foot of the stairs.

"Hey, Kit. You said you needed to talk to me?"

"Yeah, let's go in the office."

Once seated, Kit got to the point. No use dragging it out.

"Jake, I've got some bad news. The tax bill arrived and it's twice what I'd thought it'd be." She looked down, ashamed to face him. "I don't have any money, Jake." Swallowing, she looked back up. "I'm sorry." She stopped at the look on his face.

"I'm almost forty years old. It's not like I couldn't see it coming. I heard Sam bought Mrs. Lowman's land so I knew it was just a matter of time. It's not your fault." He stood up. "Daniel and I have the campsite ready and will take care of your guests as soon as they arrive."

"No. There's something else. What is it?"

Jake twisted his hat between his fingers. "It's Elena. Doc's put her on bed rest."

"Oh, no."

"She and the baby are going to be fine. I just knew if I told you, you'd feel worse than you already do."

"Anything I can do?"

"Some of Maggie's home cooking would be great."

Kit stood and smiled. "You got it. And thank you for understanding. You know I'm sick about this. I hear Dawson's hiring and that the pay's good. Promise me you'll go over there today and apply."

"I'll check it out. But, I'm more worried about you. How are you going to manage? One guide won't be near enough."

Kit smiled and shrugged. "I'll figure something out."

Jake tipped his hat and turned to go. She followed him out the back door and stood on the porch and waved to his son, Daniel, the rising senior and star football player at Sugar Creek High. She hoped he was good enough to get a scholarship. His family was going to need it.

The screen door bounced off her boot heel as it closed behind her. Stepping back inside the kitchen, she looked around the large ample space. Sam had commented that he'd had so many happy memories here. Where had the happy memories gone? It seemed lately, there was nothing but stress and anxiety. Tears filled her eyes. Sage Brush was slowly closing down. One hired hand at a time.

As promised, Kit showed up at Jake and Elena's the next afternoon with one of Maggie's best meals. Fried chicken, mac and cheese, field peas, and biscuits and gravy. After checking on Elena, and depositing an assortment of women's magazines on her bedside table, Kit put everything in the oven on low and left.

Seeing Elena propped up in her bed and unable to take care of her family had Kit worried. Her friend looked weak and uncomfortable. Suddenly, it was imperative Jake get a job at the lodge.

A half hour later, Kit pulled up into the parking lot at McCabe's Resort and in minutes was sitting in the waiting area to see Sam.

"Kit. Please come in," Sam said.

She entered the spacious office while Sam held the door for her. The smell of new leather greeted her as she stepped through the opening. His office looked comfortable but expensive. It grated on her nerves that he, a Dawson, should have all of this wealth, much of it at her own family's expense. Sam motioned her to a deep brown leather chair and took the one opposite.

"Would you like something to drink, coffee?"

"Don't get your hopes up. That's not why I'm here."

Sam shook his head, then leaned back in his chair and propped his booted feet on the coffee table. "Okay, then, why?"

Kit sat twisting her hands in her lap. "I had to let Jake go."

Something between concern and 'I told you so' filled Sam's eyes. "Why? I don't close on the Lowman deal until next month."

Kit lowered her eyes from his piercing gaze. "I don't have the money to pay him." She raised her gaze to look out the long wall of windows in his office. The view was all manicured and green and dotted with masses of colorful annuals. "I want you to give him a job." She looked at him then, hating that she was all doe eyed and pleading but couldn't help it. "I heard you were hiring. Elena's on bed rest and—"

"Done. You don't have to beg. It's me you're talking to." He clenched his jaw and took a long, slow breath. "I wish you had the same concern for the rest of the people in this town that are out of work." He lowered his feet to the floor and leaned forward placing his forearms on his thighs. "There are fifty more who have bills to pay and families to feed, Kit. But I can't hire them without that road frontage. I can't run my hotel to full capacity without it. This is bigger than both of us, more important than the past and all of its grudges. This is about saving our town. Bringing needed work to the people of this community." *And keeping you from discovering the truth of that night.*

"And putting more money in your pocket."

"Hardly. My investors are losing money every day."

"I don't care about your investors." Agitated, Kit jumped to her feet. "If I could help any other way, I would. But I won't sell. The Dawsons have all of the Kendall land they're ever going to get. It's time you accepted that. I can't help you."

She looked up at his hard features. The scowl on his face had darkened his deep blue eyes to jet black. She shrank back as he towered over her, a muscle twitching in his jaw. Raising her chin a fraction, she looked him square in the eyes. She felt like a coward but refused to let him intimidate her with that glacial stare of his. She did care for the people in Sugar Creek but she couldn't sell another inch of Kendall land, especially to a Dawson.

"Well, isn't it a good thing that I don't play by your rules. What kind of a man would I be if I refused to help Jake just to spite a Kendall?"

Kit didn't have an answer. Couldn't say a word. She turned to go. When she got to the door, her hand trembled as she reached out to grab the handle. She stepped through the opening and gently closed it behind her. Walking as quickly as she could, she was in the high-beamed foyer before the first tear fell. By the time she got to her truck, the tears ran freely.

She felt like the biggest heel. It wasn't fair. None of this was her fault. She was not about to let Sam make her feel like she was the one responsible for all of those people that needed work. After all, she wasn't the one that overbuilt. Besides, she had her own problems and people she was responsible for. And because of him she had to fire her own employees. Yet, he didn't seem to care one iota about that.

But as she drove back to the B&B, Sam's 'spite' comment began to haunt her. Was it spite to try and salvage every inch of her family's land? Was it simply a matter of having been blinded by an old grudge? She pushed the thought that he might be right to the back of her mind. It was too ugly to even contemplate.

She pulled up at Sage Brush, sniffed and blew her nose. Flipping down the visor, she checked her face. At the sight of her red nose and blotchy cheeks, she lifted her hand and fanned her face. It wouldn't do for Macy to see her like this. She'd call their mother and that would never do. No sense in worrying her. Kit wanted her to stay happy and on her honeymoon.

Kit jumped down from the truck and pushed the door to with both hands as a dull pain began to throb at her right temple. She raised her hand and pressed her fingers to the side of her head to ward off the oncoming headache. Turning, she surveyed her land. The road frontage was superior to any of the other homesteads on this highway. But compared to everybody else's acreage road frontage was about all she had. Three hundred acres was a lot to some but not to ranchers in Texas. Sections was what most of them had. So many acres that they divided it into sections, just to able to talk about it.

On impulse, she stepped off part of the property. Taking long strides, she counted, "Three, six, nine."

After marking off the strip of land, she stood contemplating what it would be like not to have it. Trying to visualize how far down it would run along her property line, she had to guess at where thirty acres would end. How deep? How wide was he talking about? Could she even part with that? Could she bear to sell a Dawson her land, even a small piece of it? Would her pride let her do it to help Sugar Creek come back to life?

Kit pushed opened the front door, just as the phone rang out from the office. She raced inside and picked up the receiver.

"Hello?"

"Don't hang up. Listen to me for a second."

"I don't have time to talk right now."

"Then you need to make time. You left before I could finish. I'm coming over."

"Not now, Sam. I have a splitting headache." She hung up the phone before he could say another word.

After taking a couple of ibuprofen, she lay on the sofa and closed her eyes. Pain seared and pounded behind her lids until she thought her head would explode. For the next half hour a battle over whether or not she should sell stormed within her. Should she, or shouldn't she? It played over and over in her mind until she thought her brain would melt.

She drifted in and out of a light sleep and began to feel a tad better. Somewhere in the house, she heard a door open and shut, then rummaging sounds from the kitchen. *Good, Macy's home.*

Kit lifted her head off the cushion. "Mace! Bring me some hot tea, will ya?" Kit yelled, then fell back against the sofa, squinting against the afternoon light now flooding through the window. Scrunching her eyes shut, she placed her forearm over her face as a sharp white light of pain shot through her temples.

The sound of footsteps and a tray being set on the coffee table broke through the throbbing and she opened her eyes. "Thanks." Kit's jaw dropped and her eyes widened.

"Close your eyes."

"I thought you were Macy."

"And your mouth." Sam had pulled a side chair up next to the couch.

Her heart thumped at his nearness. She closed her eyes and breathed in his cologne. Geranium and cedar wood, spices, sage, and cinnamon drifted over her like a warm breeze, clouding her senses.

Sam gently pressed a hot compress across her closed eyes, bringing much needed relief.

The heat penetrated her flesh instantly relaxing the tight muscles around her eyes and forehead. A soft moan escaped her lips. The gentle pressure from Sam's hand over her eyes was heavenly and soon her pain receded.

She lay there a moment longer savoring his scent and wondered how it was possible that after six years, it hadn't changed one little bit. Had he been that imprinted on her heart and mind? Yep. He'd burned into her soul like a branding iron on flesh. Leaving a permanent mark on her heart.

After the cloth cooled, he removed it, then poured her a cup of tea. Kit sat up and leaned back against the sofa. She took the cup from his hand, then blew across the liquid. After taking a sip, she looked up to find his blue eyes on her.

"Is that still how you like it? Sweet with cream?"

"Yes. It's lovely."

His lips quirked. "It's nice to have done something right."

Kit swiveled around placing her feet on the floor. She took another sip before placing the cup in the saucer.

"Look, I don't mean to sound ungracious, but say what you came to say and go."

As usual his gaze seemed to look right through her. Was that a softening in his eyes? A gentleness? Her heart betrayed her head with a treacherous tug. He leaned forward to place his cup on the table, the action causing his muscles to flex against his shirt. Resting his elbows on his knees, he leveled an intense stare at her that was impossible to ignore.

"I'm sorry I made you uncomfortable earlier. My intention was to have a friendly discussion. A chat between old friends. Turning every conversation into a confrontation isn't going to help either one of us much less Sugar Creek. Could we try to set aside our past and focus on someone other than ourselves?"

When she didn't answer, he scooted his chair closer. "Look, with the right investments and some time, Sugar Creek can become a flourishing community again. You know as well as I do that this part of Texas is perfect for what I'm trying to do. What we're both trying to do. The hunting and fishing in this area is outstanding. There's river rafting, horseback riding, and the rodeo is always a draw. Then there's camping and chuck wagon dinners. And we have the best bar-b-que in the country. And the town looks like a Hollywood set, making it a draw in its own right."

Kit took another sip of her tea, which had now gotten cold, but anything to distract from those mesmerizing, ocean blue eyes of his. She knew if she gazed into them she'd lose everything. Her self-control, her land, and most importantly, her heart. That she couldn't risk. Not again.

The strength of the pull he still had on her was undeniable. She'd been fighting it ever since he'd returned. She'd lost her heart to him once and it had taken years for her to get it, as well as her life, back to normal. But, the change in her father and the months of heartbreak mirrored in her mother's eyes was anything but normal. After they buried her father, Kit had sworn off men for good. And by golly she'd planned to keep it that way. She tossed back the last of her tea and set the cup down.

"What do you want, Sam? You already have Miss Susan's land so what are you doing here?"

He stared at her. He was being careful. She could see it in his piercing, heart-stopping stare.

Then the light dawned. "You still need my land, don't you? Buying Miss Susan's property was just a way to force my hand, wasn't it?"

He stood and gazed down at her. "I was planning to buy it at some point. Her realtor contacted my office over four months ago about purchasing it. Your refusal to sell me what I needed just forced me to buy it sooner than later. That's all. I'm not trying to hurt you Kit. If you'd just be reasonable."

"Reasonable? Why you arrogant—" She sprang to her feet, clenching her fists by her side.

"It's not arrogance. There is so much at stake, for so many people. I'll pay you more than it's worth."

"Unless you can raise the dead and erase the past, you know nothing about it's worth," she cried.

"I'm sorry." He heaved a sigh. "Look, I know what the land means to you. There's no excuse for what my father did to your family. But don't put me into the same category." He ran his hand through his thick crop of dark hair. "But your father was just as culpable as mine." He stopped, realizing he may have said too much.

"What do you mean?"

He shook his head. "I'm not interested in the past."

"You poor baby. I feel so sorry for you. The man who has everything, land, money, and all because his father was a rotten gold digger. Or should I say, oil digger."

"Give it up, Kit. You won't get a rise out of me, no matter how hard you try."

Something about his stance told her he was telling her the truth, about his father and hers. She could also tell by the stubborn jut of his chin that she'd get no more answers from him, no matter how much she tried to goad him.

Sam had been older when all of that took place. He knew something and it killed her to know that he knew it and she didn't. Pure unadulterated self-control. One of the things she'd always admired about him. Definitely one of his strengths. Until it was used against her. Then she wanted to kick something.

She marched over to the door and yanked it open. "I'll think about it," she stated abruptly. She just wanted him to leave. Or did she?

Taking a chance, she glanced at him and almost burst out laughing at the incredulous expression on his face. "You heard right. I'll think about it. That's all I can promise for now."

Sam turned out of her driveway onto the road. What just happened? He'd be darned if he knew. Lord, she was stubborn. But at least they seemed to be heading in the right direction for a change. He hadn't meant to let that slip about her father's role in the Kendalls' demise. But she'd responded to the truth of his words. She always did. He should have remembered that about her. Maybe he should tell her everything. No, he couldn't tell her. It would devastate her. As long as he was breathing, she'd never find out.

He pulled off to the side of the road and got out. Surveying the property line between their lands, he mentally marked off the acres in his head. Trying to imagine just what amount of land would be needed to make the project code-worthy.

On impulse, he strode across the parched earth ticking off the inaccurate measurement in his head.

"Counting your chickens?"

He spun around to see Kit standing about twenty yards away with her hands on her slender hips. He opened his mouth to speak, but stopped when Kit stomped toward him ready for a confrontation.

"So what do you think?" She stated in that high-pitched voice she always used when she was ticked about something.

Don't mess this up, Sammy boy.

He smiled at her, knowing how it used to make her weak at the knees. At least that's what she used to tell him. God, had it really been six years since he'd pulled her behind the tractor shed so her father wouldn't see them kissing. He remembered it like it was yesterday.

'I love you, Sammy,' she'd said with her trembling just-kissed lips. Her declaration of love and the sheer adoration that had poured from her sparkling green eyes had him dreaming of what she might give him later that evening. What twenty-four-year-old male wouldn't? But now he saw it for what it was. In that moment, she'd given him her heart. Then she'd kissed him back with an urgency and passion that'd nearly brought him to his knees. And what was his response? He'd left her the very next day.

He'd done this to her. Turned her into the sarcastic, angry, ice maiden that now stood in front of him. But, he knew his Kit was still in there, somewhere. The night at the saloon had told him that.

"Counting my chickens, huh? Is that what it looks like?"

"Yes. You always thought, 'I'll think about it,' meant 'yes'. I swear, Sam, you haven't changed one little bit."

"Oh, I wouldn't say that. I've grown older and wiser for one thing." *Especially during the past few minutes.*

"That makes two of us, sugar."

"Mmm, sugar. You haven't called me that in years."

"Six. It's been six." He watched her green eyes widen before she ground out, "Slip of the tongue. Don't expect to hear it again."

"Did you come out here to argue? If you did, I'm not interested." He removed his Stetson, then slowly, methodically, resettled it back onto his head.

She folded her arms across her heaving chest.

He knew she was trying not to lose it with him. Her face flushed red and he was reminded of the day he carried her to the creek to cool off, which immediately had him thinking of her in that lacy underwear. Blue as the sky on a summer day.

Her green eyes darkened as she shifted her weight from one slender booted foot to the other. She reminded him of a two-year-old filly ready to spring from the gates at the racetrack. Then she looked up at him and the hurt in her eyes seared him to his core. Worse, it was laced with distrust, which bothered the hell out of him. He was a lot of things but untrustworthy wasn't one of them. Needing a second to control his emotions, he turned away and looked out over the property. If only he could turn back time. If only he had been older and wiser. Maybe he could have intervened. But he was twenty-four, a young buck, full of himself and completely ignorant of the facts.

"You want to look at my land? Fine, I'll walk with you." She turned and walked away so abruptly that he had to take several quick steps to catch up with her.

"I still don't see how could you possibly need my land? Or is it . . . want? You only want it because you can't have it."

He grabbed hold of her arm and pulled her to a screeching halt. "No. That's not it at all. I need the access for city codes. Emergency vehicles have to have a road to get to the back of the property. They'll put in another fire hydrant, which is important for the safety of my guests. No one can occupy those rooms until this gets done."

She jerked her arm from his hold. "A road, uh? So, I guess that means some sort of a lease agreement wouldn't work."

Lease agreement? So, she had been thinking about it. "I'm afraid not. It simply makes more sense if I own it."

"Of course it does."

"And, financially, it's a much better deal for you."

"Of course it is." Kit heaved a sigh, then gazed out over her property chewing her lower lip. "If, and I mean, if, I were to part with thirty acres, show me what you'd need?" She threw out her arms over the area, then looked him full in the face.

He gazed deeply into her eyes and noticed, thankfully, that at least the hurt was gone. Her eyes were lovely, even with that hint of distrust still in place. They were the prettiest green. Like new growth on a holly bush in spring.

He looped his thumbs in the back pockets of his Wranglers and surveyed the property. "Let's keep walking and I'll show you what I'm thinking." They walked along the property line past the tennis courts and beyond her barn until they came to the fence that cornered her land with what used to be Miss Susan's but was now Dawson's.

"A strip of land, somewhere between the road and this corner. Give or take." Sam eyed her with bated breath. He could only imagine what was going through that short-haired, copper-covered head of hers.

"Fine." Kit folded her arms tightly around her waist. As if it had caused her great pain to say it.

He was floored. He never dreamed she'd agree so quickly. What had changed in the last fifteen minutes? *Don't question a gift horse, son. Thank her and start drawing up the papers.*

"Are you sure?"

Her head jerked up. "I'm sure. "And don't think for a

second my change of heart has anything to do with your hot compresses and tea. I'm just tired of being hounded."

"Fine."

"You'll have to pay for the survey."

"Of course."

"And I want a written agreement between us that I, my employees and guests have complete access to the Lowman land."

"You got it." But his words were spoken to thin air.

Kit had spun on her boot heals and was striding back toward her house.

Chapter 14

Three days later Kit sat across from Mr. Brown in his office. Sam sure hadn't wasted any time. The morning after he'd left, the survey was completed and agreed upon by both parties, then his lawyer drew up the sell document. And now here she was getting ready to sign thirty acres of Kendall land over to a Dawson. Had she gone completely crazy? A month ago, she'd have slit her wrists before she would've sold any more of her land, especially to a Dawson. What was it she'd said? *Over my dead body*. The words mocked as they pealed through her brain like a death toll.

"You're making a good decision, Kit. The purchase amount is more than enough to pay your loan up to date and then some. Do you have any questions before Sam arrives?" Mr. Brown asked.

"Yes, about the loan, I was hoping I'd be able to work out some sort of payment plan. My tax bill is due soon and—"

"Sam. Chris. Come in. Kit and I were just chatting."

Kit clamped her mouth shut and turned toward the door. Mr. Brown stood and held out his hand as Sam and his lawyer, Chris Billings, entered the office.

"Good morning. Brown, Kit."

Kit hated to admit it but Sam was breathtaking dressed in navy slacks and a crisp white shirt. His silver cufflinks sparked off the sunlight streaming through the window as he settled himself in the chair next to hers. Chris shook hands with Kit and sat next to Sam.

Silently, each read over the contract, signed it, and handed it back to Mr. Brown.

Kit took the check and stood, signifying her part in

the meeting was over. Wanting to deposit it as quickly as possible, she politely shook hands with each man and left. Once the deposit was made she paid her balance due and left the bank.

"Kit. Wait up."

She turned to see Sam approaching her. His long strides had him standing next to her in seconds.

"I want to thank you. I know how hard that was for you."

"Do you?"

"Look. There are a lot of families that are going to be able to pay their mortgages, put food on the table because of you. Have lunch with me."

"Look, Sam, this doesn't change anything. Plus, I'm not in a celebratory mood. I did this for Sugar Creek, not for you."

"I know that. Please have lunch with me."

"I can't. I have to go to the feed store."

"Fine. I'll go with you to the feed store."

"I don't want you to go to the feed store with me. I don't want you anywhere near me. You've gotten what you want. Now leave me alone." She stomped her foot.

"You don't mean that." He shook his head.

As Kit started to turn away, he took hold of her arms. "Can't we call a truce?"

She refused to look at him. "I've lost most of my help because of you. Now, if you'll excuse me, I have work to do." She looked pointedly at his hands that were still holding her arms.

"Can't you at least be civil?"

She pulled away. "This *is* me being civil." She turned and hurried down the street.

Sam folded his arms across his chest and watched Kit disappear down the sidewalk. Brown joined him out front and they both watched Kit enter Acme Feed and Seed.

"Congratulations, Sam. I didn't think she'd ever come round. To purchase land that already belongs to you. That's a first."

"Not a word, Brown. No one's ever to know."

"It's a fine thing you've done for her." Brown slapped him on his shoulder.

"Thanks for holding the bank vultures at bay for as long as you did. I'm sure it wasn't easy with them breathing down your neck."

"I still don't know why you just didn't pay them yourself."

"And then, what? Tell Kit she had a benevolent benefactor? She wouldn't buy it. No, this is better. As long as she still owns it on paper, that's all I care about."

"You do know this is only temporary. Her property taxes are due soon."

Sam glanced at him. "I know. I heard Kit mention it when I arrived. I thought I had this whole thing solved when her mother agreed to sell me their property two years ago. Clean. Quiet. No one need ever know. But unfortunately, Kit had other ideas."

"I know, I even suggested that she sell the whole thing and she'd have more than enough to buy another place if she wanted. I've never seen anyone work any harder to save their home. It's a crying shame what Kendall did to his family, especially to Kit."

Sam nodded and thought about his own father's hand in it. Adam Dawson knew Kendall had a gambling problem. And still let him make that damn bet. In fairness he couldn't completely blame his father. Kendall had made his own choice. He'd bet it all and lost, literally.

And then, after his father died, he found out the worst part of it, a part that would only affect Kit. He'd determined then and there he would never take part in such a deception. He couldn't live with himself knowing what was coming down the pike for her. It was unconscionable to allow Kit to believe the land was hers, land she loved, worked and poured her life's sweat into, only to find out that it would be gone on her twenty-fifth birthday.

"Don Kendall was my best friend but he had his issues and they finally caught up with him." Brown said. "I didn't like your father but even I can't lay what happened with Kendall at your father's door. The land will soon be yours whether you like it or not. Your refusal to accept it doesn't make it any less so. The codicil in your father's will only allows for a short window of time. Maybe his adding it was his way of trying to make things right in the end." Brown placed his hand on Sam's shoulder.

"Do you actually think my father felt remorse for his actions?"

"I think your leaving was harder on him than you realize. He was a scoundrel but he was a father, too. Maybe he thought you'd return to help your neighbors once you found out."

"That could be." He'd received a copy of the will in the mail two full years before his father had died, but at the time Sam had refused to read it. If he had, he'd have returned a lot sooner. As his father probably knew he would. A wave of guilt coursed through his veins. That had to be it. It was his father's way of saying, come home. He'd always communicated in a somewhat abnormal way. Never one to just get to the point. Sam had spent years trying to read his father's idiosyncrasies and peculiar nuances of communication. Always second-guessing and never quite managing to understand what Adam Dawson wanted or expected.

"You're a real gentleman to keep it from her."

Sam nodded. "Thanks, Brown, but I'm running out of ideas." He had less than a month until they celebrated their birthdays. Until then, the land still technically belonged to the Kendalls, but after that it would revert back to the

Dawsons. And until then he'd do all he could to buy the rest of the property from her while it was still hers to sell.

"Well, I've got to go back to work. Here's the deed to the thirty acres."

Sam took the document and slapped it against the palm of his hand. Thirty acres down and two hundred and seventy to go. He had no idea how to get her to sell the rest of her property but somehow he had to figure out a way.

Chapter 15

The following week turned into a hive of activity. Seemingly out of the blue, Sage Brush was over half full, and Trip and Maggie were back full time.

After waving that week's guests goodbye, Kit closeted herself away in the office with her calculator.

Maggie entered with a coffee tray to find Kit smiling.

"Lord, I haven't seen that 'good news' smile in months."

Kit beamed. "It is. Just this week's income alone will cover almost an eighth of the tax bill. And we're close to full for the next two weeks as well. If this keeps up, we'll make it." She set the calculator aside. "Boy, that coffee smells great."

"Hey, sis. Are you done with me?" Macy asked.

"Sure, honey."

Macy skipped in, hopped up on the edge of the desk, then reached for a 'cow patty'. "Maggie, you're gonna have to send me a care package after I leave. Mom never made these as good as you."

Kit watched Macy as she sat swinging her legs and licking chocolate off her fingers. She'd worked all week like a trooper. Stripping beds, washing load after load of towels and serving long hours of kitchen patrol. She gazed at her little sister, her beautiful hair reaching half way down her back. She was dressed in snug-fitting jeans and a sleeveless floral top that tied loosely in the back. So, feminine. So lovely. So Macy.

Kit stared wistfully after her. She was like Macy, once. Happy, carefree, excited about life, and a particular boy.

"So, are you going someplace with Johnny?

"Do mama birds build nests in the spring?" Macy grabbed another cookie, slid off the desk, and headed for the door. "You're sure you don't need me?"

"Do cow dogs roll in horse—?"

"Gross. Don't say it." Macy pulled a face, then bounded up the stairs.

"You should go out, too. I'll take care of everything here," Maggie said.

Kit rocked back in the desk chair. "I'm working, remember?"

"Still? You should quit that job. I don't see why you need it anymore. You've lost weight since you've taken it on, too. You're looking peaked."

"I kind of like it."

"Looking peaked?"

"Ha, ha very funny. Besides, I'm not quitting until this bill is paid." Tapping it with her index finger. "After that, I'll see."

"Too bad Jake's already over at the lodge. We sure could use him around here."

"I know, but it's not that he didn't want to come back. Apparently the resort not only pays well, but they have fabulous health benefits for their employees. With Elena on bed rest, he just couldn't give that up."

"What about his son? Maybe he could help around here?"

"That's a great idea, I'll—"

"Hello. Anyone here?"

Kit and Maggie exchanged glances. Neither had heard the front door open. Kit was the first to enter the foyer, with Maggie close behind. "Diana. What a . . . nice surprise."

"Oh, there you are. I thought I'd stop by and see if you could find room for a couple of friends of mine."

"Uh, sure." Kit thought it odd that Diana would just drop by. "But you could have just called."

"I know, but I was literally driving by, so it's not

inconvenient." She fluttered her manicured hand, releasing a heavily perfumed scent through the air.

"Anyway, our lodge is running at full capacity and I was wondering if you have any space. We're literally having to turn guests away." She chuckled.

As usual, Diana was dressed in what seemed to Kit the latest fashion. Her sleek-fitting blue suit glowed with an iridescent sheen. The image of a preening peacock came to mind.

"Really? You're full?"

"Yes, but once the road is finished and the second stage of the resort opens, we'll have plenty of space." Diana then proceeded to saunter through the downstairs as if she were looking for something.

Kit caught Maggie's incredulous expression and wanted to laugh but contained herself.

"Diana. I'm sorry, but are you looking for something?"

Diana spun on her high heels to look back at Kit. "No, I sometimes get easily distracted."

I bet you do.

"You have such a charming, cozy little place." Diana gazed around the room.

"Thank you. We like it."

"Anyway, in the meantime, my friends, Jim Thorn and Peter Addison, are two of the guests we've turned away. Not even I can get them a room." She laughed. "All they want to do is hunt and fish for a couple of weeks. They don't care a thing about luxury accommodations."

So that's what she was doing. Checking to see if the accommodations were sufficient enough.

The snub didn't go unnoticed by Kit, or Maggie either, for that matter, who huffed loudly and left the room. "I'm sorry. I'm a bit confused. Did Sam send you?" Kit asked.

"No. As a matter of fact, when I mentioned that your

B&B would be perfect for my friends, he was adamantly against it."

"Really."

"Yes. Something to do with you being, 'a single young woman on your own,' sort of nonsense. Anyway, I think it would be perfect for them. So, what do you say?"

"Well, I do have several rooms left for next week. Check-in is on Mondays."

"Good, I'll let them know."

Diana pasted on her fake smile and left.

One hour later, Kit parked her truck in the alley, then slipped through the back entrance of The Fat Canary. Mouth-watering aromas of selected meats, buttery sauces, and fresh herbs assaulted her senses making her stomach growl and since she hadn't eaten since lunch, she was suddenly ravenous.

After grabbing a quick bite in the kitchen and writing down the specials, Kit slipped into the bathroom to wash up before entering the dining area. When she leaned forward to wash her hands, she could see completely down the top of her dress. After she dried her hands, she tied the apron snugly around her waist, hoping that would cinch in the fabric, solving the problem. But it didn't. It only made the top billow out even more. She placed her hand against the fabric several times, pushing it in but it popped back out like it was spring-loaded. Kit groaned, shook her head, and left.

She was going over the specials when Sam entered with Diana and two other men. Rebecca showed them to their seats and gave them menus. Dang. Why did he always have to sit at her table? When she approached to take their drink orders she couldn't help but notice the way Sam looked at her. Was that disapproval in his eyes? She glanced away and focused on the rest of the group, only to find one of the men eyeing her in open admiration. She felt a sudden flush spread over her body under his close scrutiny. It was all she could do to keep her hands from going up to cover her cleavage.

After placing their food order, Kit grabbed a chilled pitcher of water. Just as she was about to push through the swinging door that separated the kitchen from the dining area, she spotted Sam through the glass porthole. She quickly ducked back behind the door and peeked through the opening. He was frowning and heading for the office at the back of the restaurant. Who put a burr under his saddle?

She waited for him to pass, then slipped back into the dining room unnoticed. She walked between her tables refilling water glasses, wondering what could've put Sam's nose out of joint. Probably Diana, who in that instant spoke, pulling Kit from her musings.

"Kit, these are the two men I was telling you about. Jim and Peter. Jim is a friend of mine so I can personally vouch for both of them." Diana winked at the two men. "As I told you earlier, all they want to do is hunt and fish for a couple of weeks."

Kit gave the gentlemen a brief nod, then glanced over her shoulder to see Sam in what looked like a heated discussion with Henry. She shook her head. Complaining about the food no doubt, or the service. But surely not. Her service had been impeccable. All the same, she squared her shoulders, smiled, and gave her attention to Diana and her guests.

"About the rooms, I checked and only have one for the second week. It has two beds, if the gentlemen don't mind sharing."

Diana glanced at the two men and both confirmed with a nod. "That's settled then." Diana's perfect smile sent shivers down Kit's spine. What did Sam see in that woman?

Kit glanced back down the hall. Sam was on his way back, obviously still displeased about something.

"Good. I'll see you both on Monday, then." She smiled at the three of them. "Can I get you anything else? More coffee?" she asked, just as Sam took his seat.

"No. We'll take the check," he said, obviously in a hurry to leave.

All three men reached for their wallets. Peter raised a hand and said dinner was on him so Kit took his credit card and headed for the register.

Five minutes later, Kit watched the foursome leave the restaurant as she took the dessert order from the next table.

Monday afternoon arrived and so did another houseful of guests. Kit and Macy took turns manning the welcome desk and between the two of them, got everyone checked into their rooms.

Kit had just finished with one check-in when the door opened and Diana's two friends walked in.

"Hello, I'm Jim Thorn and this is Peter Addison. We met you Saturday night."

"Yes, of course. It's nice to see you again. Welcome to Sage Brush." Kit smiled and turned the guest register around for them to sign in. The old-fashioned log sat on an antique turntable she'd found at the Sage Brush antique mall on Highway 76.

"Just like the Old West." Peter dipped the quill pen into the bottle of ink and scrawled his signature across the page.

Kit laughed. "That's the idea. We log everything into our computer after you guys are happily hunting on the property. You'll get the normal hotel printout when you check out."

"Oh, now I'm disappointed." Peter smiled.

Kit turned the book toward Jim and waited as he signed.

"Here's the weekly schedule of events," Kit handed each of the men a colorful brochure. "You can do as much or as little as you like. Trip Hunter will be taking you guys out to fly fish. You'll go out first thing in the morning and return Saturday afternoon. His office is in the barn, if you have any questions."

"We're very relaxed around here," she said as she led them upstairs. "Feel free to go anywhere you like. Oh, and the kitchen's open twenty-four-seven. Raiding the fridge is permitted and expected." She smiled and slipped the brass key into the door lock. "Here you are, Jim, and your room is across the hall, Peter. Fresh-squeezed lemonade and warm cookies will be served in an hour in the parlor. And dinner's at six."

On the way down the stairs Kit met Macy bringing up extra towels to Room 4. "When you're done, give Maggie a hand in the kitchen."

"Okay."

An hour later, while her guests mingled and enjoyed their snack, Kit made her way to the barn. A slight breeze came in from the west, bringing relief to the warm summer afternoon. Kit rounded the corner and entered the barn. As her eyes adjusted to the dim light, she heard a sound behind her, turned, and caught a movement out of the corner of her eye. Jim Thorn stepped out from the shadows.

Kit inhaled sharply and took a step backward. A prickly sensation crept over her flesh sending up a red flag. The last time Kit had felt her skin crawl was when she'd stumbled upon a nest of imported fire ants. "Jim?"

"Sorry. Didn't mean to startle you." Jim smiled and stepped toward her.

"It's okay. I thought everyone was inside for the afternoon snack. Maggie makes the best cookies this side of the Rio Grande. You're missing a real treat."

"The only treat I'm interested in is right here in this barn." His lips spread in a slow grin.

Suddenly, that red flag began to wave. "Sorry, but we're

not serving snacks out here right now." Her heart raced as she forced a smile.

"I have to say, you don't look anything like you did the other night."

Kit stared at him wondering what the heck he was talking about when the light dawned. "You mean my uniform? Not quite the thing for stripping beds and brushing down horses, I'm afraid." She forced another laugh. Even though her heart was pounding, she spoke in a light tone hoping to diffuse the situation. This guy was creeping her out. When she made a move to step around him, he blocked her path. Kit froze and her heart plummeted like the first drop on a roller coaster at the state fair.

"Kit, there you are."

Trip. Thank goodness.

Trip entered the barn, holding the reins of his horse. "Bugsy got caught on some loose barbed wire before I had a chance to pull up. Tore up his shank. He's limping pretty badly."

"Let me take a look." She pushed her way past Jim, thankful when he stepped out of the way. She bent down on her haunches and inspected the wound.

"I was checking the fence along the highway when this happened. That area still needs major repair," Trip added.

Kit stood up and patted the gelding's neck. "I'll see to it tomorrow after everyone's gone. Let's get Bugsy patched up. Excuse me, will you, Jim?" Turning her attention back to Trip, she watched Jim hover from the corner of her eye, before he quietly slipped away. Slink was more like it. Kit made a mental note to make sure Jim was never alone with Macy.

Chapter 16

The following morning, Jim, Peter, and the other men in Trip's group were the last to leave. The mules were packed with overnight supplies and plenty of good food.

Kit's blood boiled at the licentious look Jim gave her after he mounted his horse. The sooner he was gone, the better. She'd already decided not to let him and Peter stay the following week. She would have kicked him off the property sooner but since he would be away for the rest of the week, she decided to wait. Her skin crawled just thinking of that unnerving leer. The man was a male version of Diana. She could certainly see why they were friends.

The Tuesday lull allowed Kit to check the damaged fence at the north boundary. Still rattled by Jim's creepy behavior, Kit grabbed what she needed for the fence repair and climbed into the tractor. The north boundary was near the main road, completely treeless and blistering hot even at ten in the morning. She'd spotted three sections of fence that still needed mending and stopped at the farthest point so she could work her way back toward the homestead. As soon as she stepped down from the cab, the heat beat an insistent drum on the top of her head.

Great, she'd forgotten her hat. Regardless, she worked for about an hour before walking back to the cab for a cold bottle of water. In her haste to leave she'd also forgotten the ice chest. Damn. *First my hat, now the ice chest.* She wondered what else she'd forgotten. Nothing for it, she'd just have to go back to the house. She climbed up in the cab and turned the key. The sickening *chug, chug* heralded a dead battery.

"Not again." She moaned. It was a good mile and a half walk back to the house. She glanced down the road in hopes that a neighbor might be coming along, but all she saw was haze rising from the asphalt in the steaming heat. Nothing for it, she'd have to walk back. Maybe someone would come along, yet. She placed one foot in front of the other and slowly walked up the field. She knew better than to go into this blistering heat without a hat, even if a sleazy snake did have her rattled. It's not like she hadn't dealt with snakes before—the ones that crawled on their belly as well as the two-legged kind. The crunch, crunch of dry grass seemed to echo her thoughts.

Dang she was thirsty. As she trudged along she stumbled on a rock then righted herself just as she heard a car approach. It was Sam in his Audi R-8. *Oh, please, anybody but him.* The deep rumble of the sports car got louder as the sleek silver body approached and slowed to a stop.

Kit stopped and leaned against a nearby post squinting her eyes against the glare of the sun. Sam opened the door and got out.

He nodded in the direction from which she'd just come. "I take it you were the one working back there?"

Kit brushed trickles of sweat from the side of her face, then raised her hand to block out the sun. "That's not the question I was hoping to hear."

Sam shook his head. "Climb over and get in the car."

As much as she wanted to do just that, Kit stood her ground. That is if leaning exhausted against a fence post could be called standing one's ground. When she didn't move he continued.

"Only you would work in middle of the day in this drought-laden heat."

"Unlike your lady friends, I'm not afraid of hard work." She panted.

He wiped sweat from his forehead with his shirtsleeve. "It's not about hard work, it's about not killing yourself today so you can live to work tomorrow."

"My, haven't we gotten soft in our time away," she taunted with a slow grin.

Frustration rang from his voice. "Do you want a ride or not. I'm melting out here. I swear, I have a mule that's less stubborn than you." He grunted. "And look at you, only a fool would work in this heat without protection. Where's your hat?"

"If you think I'm going to continue to stand in this heat and listen to one of your lectures, you can—"

Kit sucked in her breath. She screamed, slapping frantically at her jeans.

Fire ants swarmed over her boots and legs in a mad frenzy. In less than a second. they reached her waist. In one swift action, Sam leapt over the fence, snatched her away from the ant bed and began knocking and slapping the stinging insects from her hips, legs, and thighs.

"They're underneath!" Frantic, she kicked off her boots, then unzipped her wranglers while Sam pulled them off her. Blistering whelps bubbled all over the lower half of her body.

"Where's your medicine?"

Kit's eyes flew to his. She shook her head and sobbed. "I don't have it."

He swore, scooped her up in his arms, then got her over the fence and in the car in seconds. He shot from the roadside like a bullet, only to get trapped behind a lumbering truck carrying round bales of hay.

"Come on. Come on!" He slammed his fist onto the steering wheel and swore. When the way was clear he shifted gears and maneuvered around the truck in one swift move. It was only a matter of seconds before he pulled into her driveway. He ran around the car and yanked open the door.

Her throat tightened, filling her with terror. Each laboring breath gave birth to another, then another until she felt like she would suffocate. She looked at Sam. His square jaw was clenched and the intense concern in his eyes made her want to cry. She kept her eyes on him, drawing comfort from his very presence.

"Hold on, Kit." He carried her into the house and sat her down on one of the kitchen chairs. He looked at her as he headed for the cabinet by the refrigerator.

"No not there, the other side," she choked out. Panic squeezed her chest and tears streamed down her cheeks.

At her nod, he yanked open the door and grabbed her prescription. It took all of two seconds to twist off the cap and hand her the capsule. He stood over her and waited while she swallowed the medicine with a swig of water. When she was done, he gathered her in his arms and carried her to the living room. As he laid her on the sofa, she clung to him as if her life depended on it.

"I'm calling an ambulance," he said.

"No. Wait. Give me a second." She hiccupped and swiped at her tears. "It-it takes a few minutes." She sucked in a ragged breath.

"Have you had all your shots?"

"All except the last one. Two weeks. I get the last one in two weeks."

Sam ran his hand through his hair and stood watching her. Hot tears cut down her cheeks. His own heart pounded and plummeted to his feet. He was worried sick and felt completely helpless as he waited for Kit's medicine to kick in.

Beads of sweat glistened above her upper lip. She was trembling and clearly frightened. Alarm poured from her shimmering green eyes and he ached to hold her. Instead, he sat down on the edge of the couch and grasped her trembling hands. Her grip tightened like a frightened child and he gave her hands a comforting squeeze.

"Focus on taking one breath at a time." He lifted his other hand and stroked her hair from her forehead.

"That's it. You got it. Nice and slow now. Just take your time." He spoke soothingly until her breathing became less labored and the fear in her eyes subsided.

As he gazed at her face, he thought about the first time she'd been bitten by imported fire ants. Only one percent of the population is hypersensitive to the venom and she was one of them. She was only fourteen when it happened. And at the time no one knew she was deathly allergic.

They'd been mending fences when she was attacked. She'd cried out in pain just like she did today. At first he'd told her to stop yelling and buck up. But when her breath started coming in short gasps with sweat pouring from her body, he knew it was serious. He'd swept her up in his arms and rushed her to Doc Murphy's. Sam could still see the terror in her eyes. Pleading. Begging for help before she'd gone into anaphylactic shock.

He thanked God this wasn't as bad as that'd been. Plump tears slid down her checks, he lifted his hand and gently wiped them away. "Don't cry, honey. You're going to be okay." He continued to brush her hair from her forehead until she'd grown calmer. "I'll be right back."

In seconds, he was back with a cold Gatorade and a straw. She sipped thirstily. He let her drink as much as she wanted, then set the bottle on the coffee table behind him.

"Better?"

She nodded. "Yes, thank you."

He pulled out his cell phone. "I'm calling Doc Murphy."

"No." She placed her hand on his phone stopping the call. "I know what to do."

"Are you sure? You're covered in bites." He looked intently at her bare legs. She was lying on the sofa dressed only in her sleeveless blouse and underwear. She flushed at his open perusal of her bare flesh. As she struggled to sit up he pushed her back against the sofa. "No need to get all shy on me now." He stood, gathered the lightweight afghan from the club chair, and laid it across her legs.

"So, now what?" He took her hand in his.

"I need to get in the tub. Everything I need is in my bathroom." She sat up and swung her legs off the sofa. But, before she could stand, Sam slid his arms under her legs and scooped her, afghan and all, into his arms.

"And no arguing," he said before she could protest. "I'm carrying you."

She had no intention of arguing. She slid her arms around his neck and reveled in his strength, her body quivering with his nearness. For the first time in years, she felt safe and protected and no longer alone.

Sam carried her up the stairs and gently set Kit on her bed, then went into her bathroom to fill her tub. She stood up, wrapped the afghan around her and followed him. "I'm not an invalid. I can do this."

"Sit down and take orders for once, will you? I'll get everything ready, then leave you to it."

Kit closed the toilet lid and sat down. She pointed to the cabinet under the sink. "Everything's in that plastic container."

While he gathered the items, he asked, "So how often do you go out on the property without your medicine?"

She stared at him in surprise, then sighed. "I never leave the house without it, especially if I'm working away from the homestead. I guess I've had a lot on my mind lately." She knew she'd forgotten because Jim had rattled her. But she wasn't about to let Sam know that. She noticed he'd gotten everything out and had it on the counter. "Now, pour the contents of that blue box in the tub."

"All of it?"

"Yes."

"What about this?" He held up a tube of lotion.

"That's the salve I put on after my bath. Just set it on the counter."

He did as he was told and in a few minutes the tub was ready for her. He stood and looked down at her. "Promise me you won't forget anymore."

She stared up into his amazing eyes. His genuine concern warmed her heart like sunshine after a cool rain. The feeling caught her off guard and touched her in a secret place in her heart. "I promise."

For just a moment her eyes locked with his and communicated a silent message she, for one, wasn't ready to openly admit to.

"Leave the door cracked, okay? Just in case you need something."

She rolled her eyes and shooed him from the bathroom, then left a crack in the door as he requested.

After taking off her blouse, she slipped out of her underwear, then stepped into the soothing medicated water.

"Are you in yet?" he shouted from her bedroom.

"Yes." She sank beneath the warm blanket of water and lay back against the white porcelain.

"Okay, keep talking to me so I'll know you're all right."

"I doubt there's any risk of me drowning."

"I don't care, keep talking."

"Fine. What do you want to talk about?" She waited and when he didn't speak, she called to him. "Sam?"

"How come Trip wasn't taking care of the fence? Don't you have enough to do running the B&B without adding fence work to the list?"

"Trip's out with the guests until Saturday. And as you saw for yourself, the fence couldn't wait."

Kit sank lower into the water. "You sure ask a lot of nosy questions," she mumbled.

"I heard that."

She smiled. Sam was clearly concerned for her and her toes tingled with the thought. She felt her eyes widen. Why in the heck would her toes be doing that? She was warming up to him again, *that's why.*

Admit it. He lassoed your heart the moment you saw him at the hotel. That was the real reason she'd turned and ran. She'd told herself it was because she hated him. Hating him was her armor. Her protection. As long as she hated him, she couldn't be hurt. But as it turned out, hate was a sorry excuse for real protection. It made her armor weak and brittle, susceptible to cracking under pressure. She'd better watch it or the weight of his masculine presence and his most recent attentiveness would have her in pieces.

Sam slipped his phone from his pocket, punched in a number, and pressed 'send'.

"Hey, Jake. Grab a couple of the guys and fix the fence along Kit's north boundary."

"Are you talking about that stretch along the road?" Jake asked.

"That's the one."

"I'm on it, boss."

Sam pocketed his cell and stood to his feet. He snuck up to the door and peeked inside. She was lying back in the water staring at the ceiling, a slight smile hovering on her lips. Good, she hadn't drowned. He left the door ajar and tiptoed back to the bed, positioning himself so he could see her face. He locked his hands together in his lap and watched her. She was obviously daydreaming about something. From the expression on her face, it was clearly a pleasant memory. He was still concerned about her and had every intention of calling Doc Murphy to tell him what had happened. Relieve his own worries, if nothing else. He dropped his head in his hands. Even after all these years, thinking back over those first critical minutes with her sent his heart into overtime. There'd only been a few times in his life when he'd experienced real fear, and that was one of them. Doc had told him if it hadn't been for his quick response, she'd have died that day. Today's reaction was not as severe, but just a frightening.

She was saying something. "What was that?" He asked.

"I said some of us don't have five stars stamped on their fancy hotel brochures. Some of us can't hire throngs of people. Oh, and here's one for you . . . some of us actually *have* to work for a living."

He could see her rolling her eyes and he smiled. She was fine. Back to her sweet, snarky, adorable self.

Heaven help him, it took fire ants to reveal what his heart had been trying to tell him for weeks now. Getting smacked upside the head with a two-by-four couldn't have gotten his attention any better. He'd been so obsessed with getting his way he'd forgotten the most important thing.

He gazed at her through the crack in the door and watched her with this new realization. His affection had grown into this sweet maddening frenzy that his heart could no longer deny. The way she leaned back against the tub accentuated her lovely face, slender neck, and her white shoulders. His eyes moved to her sweet mouth and her perfect nose. Her short wet hair spiked up in an odd but appealing way and that smattering of gold dust across her nose made him suck in his breath. The combination of her bare shoulders and what lay right below the water's surface sent tremors down his spine. She was exquisite. A sexy, little tomboy.

She'd closed her eyes. "Hey, don't fall asleep."

"No chance of that with your constant yapping." Irritation rang from her voice, causing him to smile.

"How long do you have to stay in there?"

She didn't open her eyes. "Hmm, just a few more minutes." She sighed, drowsily.

While he waited, he reached over and picked up a photo from her bedside table. It was a picture of Kit and Macy with Daisy and her new husband. It looked like it had been taken at their wedding. Daisy was still an attractive woman. Good for her for finding love again.

"Hey, what's your mom's husband's name?" When she didn't answer, he glanced back toward the opening. Kit wasn't there. Thinking she'd slipped under the water, he jumped up and jerked open the door.

Kit screeched. She was right in the middle of drying off and quickly covered her wet naked body. Her eyes were as big as saucers. "Get the heck out of here!"

He looked away but not before he caught a glimpse of her lovely backside in the mirror. He couldn't help it. He raised his eyes and stole a quick glance in her direction. She was fumbling with the towel and frantically tucking it around her slender body.

"I'm sorry. When I didn't see you, I thought you'd fallen asleep."

"How would you know?" She suddenly stopped, her eyes widening. "You were watching me?"

"I was only checking on you. I didn't see a thing." He fought like the devil not to smile, but totally lost that battle with himself.

"Oh, yeah. Then why are you grinning like a loon?" She gripped the towel tightly around her.

Her neck and shoulders glistened with bath water. That, coupled with the pink flush of embarrassment now covering her adorable face, had him wishing he wasn't such a gentleman. He wouldn't be a man if he didn't wish that towel would slip down just a little bit lower, preferably around her ankles. He shook his head ever so slightly. Well, he could dream, couldn't he?

"Was I grinning?" He deliberately put on an innocent expression.

Kit slapped her free hand against his chest and shoved him from the bathroom.

With the door fully slammed in his face, he could now smile as broadly and roguishly as he pleased.

Saturday night Kit slipped into her black dress and heels. Even though the bites on her legs were almost gone and barely noticeable, she dabbed on a bit of makeup, anyway.

She passed by the repaired fence on her way into town and wished like the dickens Sam hadn't sent his men to fix it. Now she felt even more obligated to him.

She arrived at work to find the boss had ordered new dresses and shoes for the girls. The dresses were still black but not near as low cut and the shoes were low heeled strappy sandals that were much more comfortable and still just as pretty. Kit was elated and wondered why the change. She suddenly remembered Sam's comment about it a few weeks ago. Amazed at the influence he obviously had with the owner.

She followed Pam into the bathroom to wash up before the dinner guests arrived.

"Do we put these on now?" she asked.

"No, Henry wants us to try them on at home before cutting the tags off. See you out front."

After slipping the outfit back in the garment bag, Kit turned from right to left in front of the mirror for a last glance before washing her hands and heading to the kitchen. She'd lost a couple of pounds over the past couple of weeks so the dress fit even looser. She'd even pinned the shoulders up hoping that would help but it didn't. Oh well, she only had to live with it one more evening.

She was going over the specials when Sam entered with Diana, Jim, and Peter. She was surprised to see Jim and Peter with them, as her guests usually attended the chuck wagon cookout.

She so did not want to wait on Jim.

Monday night, before the hunters were to leave on Tuesday, Jim had cornered her in the upstairs hallway as she was making her way to her bedroom. But before he could utter a word, Peter came up the stairs behind her with instructions from Trip as to what they'd need to pack for the four-day excursion. Thankful for Peter's timely interruption, she wished them goodnight, then made her escape to her bedroom.

She sighed. Even though she felt safe at the restaurant, Jim's disgusting behavior still unnerved her.

She watched, as they followed Rebecca to one of the tables. Kit held her breath. Hot dang! She danced a jig. Rebecca seated them at Pam's table.

Rebecca then led a nice middle-aged couple to her table. Kit fought back the urge to hug Rebecca and, except for those blasted high heels, would have skipped over to them to take their order. With a smile of complete satisfaction, she watched Rebecca hand out the menus.

After that, the rest of the evening flew by. Saturday nights were always busy and by the time Kit hobbled out the door, her feet were killing her. She leaned against the doorjamb, slipped off her heels, and gingerly walked the rest of the way to her truck. Just as she was about to reach the vehicle, a sharp pain shot through the ball of her foot. She winced, sucking in a sharp breath. "Dang! What the heck?" She hopped the last few feet before falling against the truck door.

Balancing against the Chevy, she raised her foot and leaned over to inspect it. A thumbtack had sunk deep into her flesh. With her teeth clamped together, she gingerly worked it out. As she opened the door her mind raced over to when she'd gotten her last tetanus shot. Definitely within the last few years so she was okay. She climbed in and tossed the tack under her seat.

"Blast it! I forgot the dress." She started the truck, then pulled up in front of the restaurant and got out. When banging on the front door drew no response, she cupped her hands against the window and peered through the glass.

"Shoot." It was already dark and everyone was gone.

"Forget something?"

Kit spun around. "Jim. What are you doing here? Where are the others?" Sudden panic rose in her throat.

"They're over at the saloon. I stepped out for a smoke and spotted you. Sorry if I startled you." The gleam in his dark eyes suggested otherwise.

"Oh, that's okay. I'd forgotten something but everyone's gone home." Heart pounding, she backed toward her Chevy.

His eyes slowly raked over her retreating figure, his gaze settling on her cleavage. "Did you think you could sidestep me by having me seated at another table?"

Kit didn't answer, but just as she reached for the handle, he grabbed her arm.

"You look terrific." He slid clammy fingers down her bare arm.

"This is so much better than those baggy plaid shirts you wear. Lord, woman, I swear you could make a bulldog break his chain."

Her eyes shot from her arm to his ruddy face. His smile had turned into a leer. Her heart raced. Double-time. Triple time. Trying to calm herself, she sucked in a breath. She needed to diffuse this. She could tell he'd been drinking.

That coupled with his obvious tendency toward lecherous behavior made for a very unpleasant situation.

She thought she'd heard a door opening somewhere. Frantic, she looked around to see if anyone was on the street.

"Jim, please let go of my arm." Her voice sounded calm to her own ears but the *thud, thud* of her heart beating against her ribs almost had her panting for breath.

"Sure, sweetheart. But how about a little kiss first?" he slurred.

"It's late and I have to teach Sunday school in the morning."

"Sunday school? I didn't think churches let girls like you get anywhere near them." His hungry eyes darted back at her low cut front as he pulled her roughly to his chest.

She'd had enough. Clenching her teeth, she jerked her arm from his hold. "Don't bother coming back to Sage Brush. I have no room for the likes of you."

Anger lit his bloodshot eyes. Alarmed, Kit shrank away from him. Just as she tried to make a run for it, he pressed closer, pinning her against the truck. She drew back, sickened by his hot breath, the stench of alcohol forcing her head to one side. Her stomach rolled. Her heart beat in a sudden, irregular rhythm, nearly suffocating her in its intensity.

"You're a fighter. I like that in a woman. But, you shouldn't flaunt your wears, sweetheart."

"Jim, please. You're drunk." She held her body rigid, prepared to fight until her last breath if she had to. Some instinct told her to keep him talking. "It's the uniform." Oh God, why was she trying to explain anything to him?

Before Kit uttered another word, a pair of powerful hands came out of nowhere, gripped Jim by the shoulders and flung him off her.

Her own body jerked in response. She watched wide-eyed as Sam reared back before flattening Jim to the pavement. Sweet relief flowed over her like the banks of a river in a storm.

Neither she nor Jim had noticed Sam's approach.

Sam then reached down, gripped Jim by the shirt collar, and pulled him to his feet. Yanking him around, Sam planted another blow against the man's jaw. Jim floundered like a Bobblehead before sprawling face down in the street.

Adrenalin kicked in and it took every bit of Kit's strength not to sink to her knees. Right then, all she wanted to do was collapse into Sam's arms. The sudden longing for him to hold her sent shock waves through her system. Reaction set in and even though she tried to force her legs to hold steady, they began to shake. She was thankful she'd had the truck at her back.

"Are you all right?" Concern mingled with anger fired out of his eyes as he took hold of her.

Kit nodded and stared at his broad shoulders. Holding her body rigid, she vowed not to lean her head against him. No matter how tempting.

"You don't have to be so tough, you know." Making it obvious to Kit that he knew what was going through her head.

Oh yes, I do.

"Good heavens. What happened?" Diana ran up to them as Peter stopped to help Jim up.

"Ask your friend." Sam looked at Diana as he opened the passenger door for Kit to get in.

Kit shuddered at the anger she saw in his eyes, turning the dark ocean depths to near black. She'd only seen that look of rage once before. The night she'd found him with his father and hers at the lodge. Kit shook off the memory and brought her attention back to the present.

Diana turned and spoke quietly to the two men.

Peter nodded and took Jim with him.

"I'm calling the police." Sam said.

Kit laid her hand on Sam's arm. "No. Please. I don't want that."

Sam stroked her cheek. "Okay. If you're sure." He pulled his car keys out of his pocket and handed them to Diana. "I'm taking Kit home, I'll see you tomorrow."

Diana leaned toward Kit, resting one manicured hand along Kit's arm. "I'm so sorry. That's not at all like Jim to act that way. I can't imagine what came over him?"

Kit stared at her. She couldn't shake the feeling that Diana knew exactly what Jim had been up to.

Sam shut her door, walked around to the driver's side, and got in. He started the ignition but sat waiting for Diana to get to his car. Kit leaned her head back and looked over at him. He was staring straight ahead, his jaw clenched and his hands white against the steering wheel.

"I guess I should thank you."

"You guess?" Wide-eyed, he turned toward her.

She spread her hands in appeal. "That didn't come out right. Thank you. I mean it. It's just . . . I had it under control."

"It sure as hell didn't look like it from where I stood."

She sighed. "I'm grateful. Really, I am. Especially after what you did for me yesterday, but did you have to hit him twice? He was down the first time."

Sam shook his head. "You're something, you know that? Well, I'm sorry I didn't stop to ask your permission on how to proceed. Next time, I'll wait and let you tell me how you'd like me to handle the situation." He heaved an impatient sigh. "Kitten, there are some things you've yet to learn about men. Just because on most days you dress and act like one, doesn't mean you know squat about them." He started the engine and pulled away from the curb.

An uncomfortable silence filled the vehicle. Is that how he saw her? The thought cut her to the quick and had her heart plummeting. Of course that's how he saw her. It's how Maggie and Macy saw her, too. She looked down at the sleek black dress. Her flesh exposed in all the wrong places. Or, right places, depending on who was doing the looking. She didn't look like a man now.

"I guess this getup didn't help matters. Maybe if I'd been wearing something else."

"He raked his fingers through his hair and stared at her in disbelief. "Honey, you could have been wearing a sack and he'd have acted the same way."

Suddenly, Kit began to shake. Her entire body trembled like a tiny earthquake.

Sam swore, pulled to a stop, then gathered her into his arms. He was the biggest cad. This was no time for a lecture. He held her tightly against his chest. The feel of her trembling body tore him up, filling him with regret. Over lost years and his father's irrevocable actions. But he was here and it was now and she was safely tucked in his arms.

"It's reaction, honey. You'll be okay." Hugging her close, he spoke tenderly, his chin grazing the top of her head. "Everything will be okay."

"I thought . . . if you hadn't come." Her voice broke and she sobbed against his shoulder.

"Listen to me. You're not responsible for Jim's actions. And I won't have you thinking it. The guy is pond scum."

"Manure on boot heels," she whispered brokenly into his shoulder.

"Yes, that, too, sweetheart."

When he called her sweetheart, she cried even harder. Seconds later, he got a muffled squeak against his chest followed by a nod. He held her for a few minutes longer until he felt her tremors cease. Even then, he didn't let her go. He knew in that instant, he could go on holding her forever.

When she pushed against him, pulling out of his hold,

ache sure and solid filled him. He watched her swipe at her tears, then settle herself back in the passenger seat.

Compassion filled him along with a sudden self-hatred. Nothing was going as he had hoped. He reached over and gently tilted her chin with his hand but she kept her eyes lowered.

He pressed his lips together and studied her. She sat perfectly still clutching her high heels in her lap. The jet-black fabric of her dress framed her smooth white skin to perfection. Even her boy haircut and tear-streaked face couldn't hide the fact that she was all woman. In fact, it was quite a combination. With her skirt inched high upon her thighs, revealing a pair of long shapely legs, it was all he could do to keep his own hands off her.

If she could only see what she looked like through a man's eyes. Did she have any clue how gorgeous she was? He gazed at her beautiful face, her slender neck, and her perfect body. She was a knockout.

He rubbed his fingers across his forehead. "Why aren't you wearing your new dress?"

She lifted her green eyes to his face. Her anguished expression tugged at his heart. "How do you know about the new dress?" Her voice was low, raspy, almost a whisper.

"He had to tread carefully. "Henry mentioned it." He stopped, hoping she wouldn't ask any more questions.

Kit nodded. A shudder ran through her body, as she grew calmer. "You don't have to take me home, you know."

"Of course, I do. What kind of cowboy do you think I am?" He felt his eyes soften as he looked at her.

"Are you a cowboy? You look and act awfully citified since you came back."

"Except for my right hook, you mean." Then he playfully landed one on her upturned chin.

"Except for that." She sniffed, smiling through her tears.

"Here." He pulled a handkerchief from his pocket and handed it to her.

She eyed it uncertainly.

"Don't worry, it's clean."

Kit pursed her lips, took the white cotton square from his hand and waved it through the air. "Like I said, citified." She proceeded to blow her nose, then clutched the handkerchief in her fist. He watched as she sat twisting and untwisting one end of it around her finger.

"Are you okay now?"

She nodded.

He put the truck in gear and continued down the road. Diana's taillights had long since disappeared in the distance. He glanced over at Kit. Her tears had washed away most of her makeup revealing her freckles. Except for that dress, she looked like a little girl sitting there next to him.

It was no use in denying he was still attracted to her. He fought the sudden urge to stop the truck and pull her back into his arms. Holding her had been sheer heaven.

The day he pulled her behind the barn to kiss her had been one of the last happy memories he'd had with her. The thought of her warm loving kisses still lit a fire in his belly and more importantly, his heart. But would she ever forgive him for leaving her like he did?

The night she came to the lodge, she'd no idea what had just happened. No idea that by morning her whole world would change. Thing is, he didn't know it either. And didn't find out the full extent of what had happened that night until his father had died two years ago. And that's when he put his plan in motion. To refurbish the lodge, to save the town and her.

Her reaction to his return had him treading carefully. One false move and he'd mess up any chance he might ever have with her again.

"I'm sorry for what happened tonight. My instinct about that guy was right."

"I get the feeling, Diana was in on it. Why do you even have her working for you? I don't get it?"

"I'm beginning to wonder the same thing myself. I met Diana four years ago when we both worked at the Ritz-Carlton in Dallas. I was one of the managers and she was the guest relations officer." He slowed the truck and turned right at the next corner. "Working with Diana, I quickly learned the real person behind the facade. But, we worked well together and she is very good at her job. So, when I refurbished the lodge, it made sense to bring her along."

"Did you date her?"

"Not in the traditional sense. But, she always made it clear that she'd like to." He glanced at her. "I feel badly about tonight. Jim and Peter are friends of Diana's and that's the only reason I let them join me this evening."

Kit shifted in her seat. "Is that the reason you didn't want them at my place?"

"They're staying at your place?" His head snapped around at her words.

She nodded. "Diana came over last week and asked if I had any rooms."

Sam stiffened. "Did she?"

"Yeah, she said the lodge was full and made it clear you didn't like the idea of them staying at my place."

He pressed down on the clutch then shifted gears. "I see. So you put them up to spite me?"

Kit shrugged. "Your interference angered me and I wasn't about to let you tell me who I could and couldn't have staying on my property. And while we're on the subject, just because I sold you a few acres, doesn't give you any rights to the rest of my land and it certainly doesn't mean I answer to you. You know I wouldn't work for you if my life depended on it."

"I'm well aware of that." He sighed. "In my defense, I didn't want them at your place because I didn't trust Jim. Peter seemed to be okay but I could tell Jim was bad news. Over the past few weeks, I've recommended your place to several guests we've had to turn away. Diana knows better than to send you someone I hadn't personally recommended. She put you in a dangerous situation and I'm truly sorry."

"You don't need to apologize. It wasn't your doing."

"One of my employees put you in harm's way. As owner of the lodge, that makes me responsible."

This whole thing was his fault and he knew it. If he'd known what havoc that little black dress would wreak, he would never have okayed it for the female employees at his restaurant. The dresses had been Diana's idea. What was it he'd just said to her? As owner, that made him responsible. He clenched his jaw. There'd be hell to pay when she found out she *was* working for him.

Chapter 17

Kit was up early and entered the kitchen to find Tess had already made coffee.

"Hey, I should be waiting on you."

"No way." Tess smiled and handed Kit a large mug of coffee. "Go prop your feet up and enjoy. Breakfast will be ready shortly." She shooed Kit from the kitchen.

Kit curled up on the living room sofa thankful the guests didn't arrive until Mondays. It was nice having a day between arrivals, especially after the events of last night. A shudder ran through her at Jim's aggressive behavior. What was wrong with people? She shook her head, blew over the hot liquid, and gingerly took another sip.

Trip and Tess had spent the night at Sam's request. At first, Kit had balked at the idea, not wanting to disturb them at such a late hour. But Sam had insisted, refusing to leave her alone.

"Fine, I'll call Maggie," she'd said.

"No. I want a man here in case Jim shows up. It's either Trip or me, take your pick."

She picked Trip.

To be honest, it was comforting having Trip and Tess on the premises. The shocked, wide-eyed expression on Macy's face when she'd found out made Kit thankful she and her sister didn't have to spend the night alone. Trip and Tess had been so angry at what had happened to her, too. Especially Trip, who upon his arrival, promptly packed up Peter's and Jim's belongings and had them waiting at the front door for pick up by the bellman Sam had scheduled for that purpose.

Sam, as usual, had thought of everything. She'd have to be blind not to notice how protective he had become. As if he had a vested interest in her. The thought warmed her like one of Maggie's hot biscuits. Kit shifted positions on the couch, wincing at the sharp pain in the back of her neck. Placing her hand on the offensive area, she gently pushed and pulled along the tender spot. She'd only had a massage once in her life and boy could she use one now. Drawing her knees to her chest, she sat back against the cushions and took another sip of coffee.

Tess entered the living room with Kit's breakfast on a tray, disrupting her thoughts.

"Oh, you didn't have to do that." Kit unfolded her legs and started to stand.

"No, don't get up," Tess stated in her cheery voice, then placed the tray on the coffee table.

"You're spoiling me. That's Maggie's job, you know." It was so sweet of Tess to fuss over her.

"I know, but it's my turn, today." Tess chuckled and left Kit to her breakfast.

About halfway through the meal, Kit sat back with a jolt. Sunday. She glanced at the wall clock. Eight-thirty. If she hurried, she could just make it to her Sunday school class. She scarfed down the rest of her breakfast, then made her way to the kitchen.

Tess had just grabbed hold of the coffee pot when Kit entered. "You ready for a refill?" she asked.

"Sorry, Tess, but I forgot. I have to teach Sunday school."

"Why don't you let me take your class today? Macy's on board with it."

"She's up?"

"Yes. She's already had breakfast and just went up to get ready for church."

"Oh." She sighed, then smiled sheepishly. "I'd love a

break, if you're sure you don't mind. I'm beat actually and could use a lazy morning."

"No need to apologize. You've had a rough night and you deserve a quiet morning to yourself." Tess picked up Kit's empty coffee mug, refilled it, then handed it back to her. "There. Now go relax," she commanded.

The flat highway was a perfect spot to accelerate the R-8. Sam hadn't had the car out for what he termed a real drive, since he'd spotted Kit walking along her fence. And after what he went through with her, all thoughts of fast driving fled. But he needed to think and there wasn't a better way to clear the cobwebs than driving this beauty. So this morning, he headed out the resort entrance in search of a smooth surface where he could let his car and his thoughts battle it out.

He traveled along Route 17 and turned right at the crossroads on Highway 71. This was more like it – a nice, long, flat stretch of road with curves in the distance. He pressed the accelerator. Forty, forty-five, fifty. The needle on the odometer moved across the numbers in seconds until the yellow line in the center of the highway blurred into insignificance.

With each acceleration he thought of nothing and no one, but Kit. Anyone who knew the truth could not question his motives where she was concerned, they had been pure enough. But relationships were built on trust and he'd put off telling her the truth long enough. Adrenalin rushed through Sam's veins and it wasn't from the speed of his R8. He loved her. Loved her tender heart, her husky voice, and her sweet lips against his.

Power lines, trees, and fences flew by at lightning speed. His eyes riveted and focused, recorded everything he passed.

As he approached the first bend in the road he slowed slightly then accelerated through the curve. The needle hit eighty, eight-five, ninety. At the next bend, he slowed again and made the loop to head back to town.

He was nervous as hell, but it was time to have a heart to heart with her. Kit wasn't a fool and if he ever wanted to have a chance with her, he had to tell her everything. He knew she still didn't fully trust him and he dearly wanted her trust.

But there was something else he needed to take care of. Something he'd been thinking about for weeks. He pulled out his phone and dialed his lawyer, Chris Billings.

A sudden knock at the door jarred Kit from her slumber on the couch. She stretched and looked at her watch. Eleven-thirty. Sliding to her bare feet, she walked over to the door and opened it. Her heart flipped a somersault. Sam stood behind the screen looking down at her. He smiled slowly and laid a look on her that said he knew all of her secrets. The sparkling intensity in his blue eyes took her breath away.

"May I come in?"

The sound of his deep voice broke the spell and she pushed open the screen door. "Since when do you ask?" She couldn't help herself and smiled up at him. He responded with a flash of even white teeth that made her knees buckle.

"Would you like some coffee?" she asked as she stepped aside for him to enter.

"Sure, that'd be great," he said, then followed her into the kitchen.

She busied herself with the simple task, fully aware his eyes were on her. She glanced back over her shoulder and he was leaning against the doorjamb, hands stuffed into his pockets, watching her. His expression was pleasant but his eyes were intense and watchful, but in a good way, as if he couldn't get enough of her. Breathless, she handed him a large mug. "Cream, no sugar, right?" She knew perfectly well how he took his coffee, but felt the need to say something. She gulped nervously, poured herself a cup, then walked back to the living room.

Kit watched Sam lower himself into her father's favorite chair, surprised his action didn't bother her one iota. For some reason this pleased her and she was suddenly very, very happy.

Sam took a sip, then placed his mug on a side table. "Kit, there's something I need to tell you." Sam became serious and was watching her intently.

Uh oh. So much for being happy.

Sam watched Kit's bright eyes go from luminous to wary. Maybe telling her everything about her father and that night wasn't such a good idea after all. Not usually this indecisive, he stood up, took one step, then sat on the sofa next to her. He swallowed, took a deep breath, opened his mouth, then clamped it shut again. She sat waiting, looking up at him, innocent of the facts. Facts and information he didn't have the courage to reveal. At least, not until he had to.

She was emotional about her land and her home, as she should be. Emotions and love went hand in hand, right? As he sat there, the idea he'd run by Chris earlier mushroomed into greater clarity.

He'd have to come at the problem from an emotional point of view. He didn't need to take Sage Brush to save it. He needed to team up with her. Not buy it, but buy into it. It just might be possible his investment in her property would negate that part of his father's will. He'd have to check with Chris to be certain, but if he became her partner, then hopefully, she'd never have to know about the codicil. She would still own half, if not most of Sage Brush, run it as always but with him being part owner. It just might work.

He reached for her hands and turned her toward him.

She shifted in her seat, never once taking her eyes from his face.

"Kit." He cleared his throat. "You and I are both having our own particular difficulties, right?"

She nodded but he could see a skeptical gleam in her eye.

"I have a proposition for you. Now hear me out," he added, when she opened her mouth to speak.

"All right." She continued to gaze up at him.

"What do you say we pool our resources?"

An incredulous expression crossed her face. "I don't have any resources. At least not financial."

"The financial resources would all be on my end. Your asset is your property."

Kit pulled on her bottom lip and sat waiting for him to continue.

"Would you consider letting me buy into Sage Brush as a junior partner?" He watched her smooth forehead crease into a frown. "It would still be your business because you'd still own most of it. You'd run it and manage it as before. Nothing would change there. My contribution would only be financial."

Kit's eyes widened and her mouth flopped open. She just stared up at him.

"Think of it. You'd have enough money to update the electrical, the plumbing, and anything else you needed, adding modern conveniences without ever robbing Sage Brush of its integrity."

Disbelief poured from her eyes like honey from a jar. "Sam . . . I-I don't understand? What are you talking about? Why are you offering this?"

"You'd also have enough to pay your taxes." He added, hoping to veer her away from the 'whats' and 'whys'.

Kit's eyes flattened to slits. "What do you get out of this? What's in it for you?"

She was skeptical. All right, he could handle skeptical. He inched closer to her on the sofa. "Remember when I talked about how people want both country cooking and five-star cuisine?"

"Yeees," she said, still eyeing him doubtfully.

"Well, between your place and mine, we can do that. We can give our guests a choice between cozy, family-centered vacations or sophisticated, resort-style vacations. Sage Brush is fresh-baked cookies and chintz. McCabe's Resort is bourbon and leather. Both can be five-star experiences. I think anytime you can give options, is a win-win." As he spoke, he watched Kit's eyes light up like fireworks on the fourth of July. Hope soared in his chest but just as quickly disappeared when her expression sobered.

"I don't know. Your offer is certainly generous. In fact, way too generous." She grabbed a peppermint from the candy dish, unwrapped it, and popped it in her mouth.

He waited, giving her a chance to think, and watched as she rolled the candy from one side of her mouth to the other.

Suddenly, she raised her eyes to his and gave him one of her challenging, chin raising looks. "Some part of me thinks you're up to something. As appealing as it is, I can't help but feel like you have an ulterior motive."

He clenched his jaw. This was not what he wanted to hear. He ran his hand around the back of his neck.

"Sorry, but you can't blame me, can you?" She crunched down on the red and white confection.

He sighed inwardly. She was so close. He couldn't lose her now. He lifted his hands to cup her smooth face. "Don't you think it's time you trusted again? Trusted me?" Then he lowered his head and kissed her. Her warm lips, mingling with sweet peppermint and cloves, freely met his. And when she kissed him back, his heart rocked. He lifted his head, looked into her eyes and saw a 'yes' in their depths. Elated, he reached into the candy dish, unwrapped a peppermint, and popped the candy into his mouth.

"Mmm, these *are* good."

God, she loved the way his eyes crinkled at the corners when he was happy. He was so handsome, sitting there, all six-foot-two of him, making her heart sing again. She'd fought it, of course. Hating that it was him bringing her back to life. He'd always had a way with her. Could melt her with just one glance of those amazing eyes of his. But, trust him? That was something else. She took a deep breath and sat up straighter.

"Okay. But before we go any further, I need to know about that night."

She'd surprised him. This he wasn't expecting. She could see it in his eyes and his sudden sober expression.

"You're right, you should know." He reached across her lap and took hold of one of her hands. "But first, tell me what you remember?"

She brushed her bangs from her forehead. "I remember coming to the lodge to look for my father. He'd been gone for hours. Mom was concerned about him and asked me to go over and check with you guys, to see if you'd seen him. She said Dad had been with Mr. Dawson a lot lately and figured that's where he was. If you recall, it was pretty late. I looked for you when I arrived but I couldn't find you. So I went to the office and right as I got there, Dad flew out and ran past me. The look on his face . . . it was awful. And then I saw you and Mr. Dawson."

She pulled her hand from his and looked down at her lap. "You were so angry. Both of you." She licked her lips and looked back up at him, then shrugged. "When you didn't say anything, I ran after my father." Kit bit down on her lower lip. "Then, the next day you were gone." She continued to stare at him. She knew her eyes questioned, begged for answers, but she didn't care.

Sam reached for her hand again. "Yes, I was angry. But not at you."

"That's not what it looked like to me. You just stood there, eyes blazing, and didn't say a word. That was my last memory of you, Sam."

"I know and I'm sorry. I was angry with my father for what he'd done and with yours for being such a fool. After you left, my dad and I had a huge fight. I begged him not to go through with it. Motivated by greed and his own desire to acquire personal wealth, he refused to listen. So, I packed a bag and left. But I never meant to hurt you." He gently grabbed her forearms. "Please believe that. I acted in the moment and in anger." He sighed and cupped her face in his hands. "I was young, Kit. And, frankly, I needed to get away from my father and take responsibility for my own life. I needed to grow up."

"Believe it or not, I understand that. It's just the rest of it that still hurts. What your father did to mine. It was, it was—"

"Underhanded and wrong. I know. But legal, I'm afraid. I know that doesn't make it any less despicable. It's haunted me for years."

"Haunted you?" A sarcastic cackle shot from her lips. "Well, it destroyed my father." She took a deep breath and shook her head. "Do you have any idea what it did to him when oil was discovered on property he no longer owned?"

"I can't say that I do. Although I can imagine the hurt, the outrage."

"He could have gotten out of debt. Become financially secure."

Sam took Kit's hands in his. "Only if he could have gotten to the oil. But he didn't have the money or the resources to drill the land. And my father did offer to pay him a percentage. What happened was unfortunate, terrible, but your father should have taken the money—"

"Money. It all comes back to that, doesn't it?"

"No. It does not." Sam sighed heavily. "Believe it or not, for the past couple of years I've tried to make it right, especially since I've come back."

"How? By pestering the heck out of me at every turn?" She folded her arms across her chest.

He was looking at her with those gorgeous eyes, then that killer smile sprang to his lips, unraveling her last ounce of reserve against him. How could she not trust that face? The face of her childhood crush. The face of her teenage sweetheart. Could she let go of the hurt and the pain of the past? She wanted to. Badly. Lord, he was hard to resist. Sitting here, all flesh and blood. Real and alive, offering her a way out of her financial problems. Problems he had caused, but if it hadn't been him, it would have been someone else. Maybe her father should have taken the money Adam Dawson had offered. Her dad was the worst at holding grudges. If not for that, he might be alive right now.

Maybe it was time for her to forgive and say yes to the offer of help as well. Suddenly, she knew that she'd probably been blind to many things, and that her heart had held, petted and coddled her hurts and disappointments far too long. For the first time she saw the ugliness of it. The wasted years in nurturing her sad little grudge.

Yes. She'd do it. She'd accept his offer. Suddenly, it was as if her forgiving heart opened a door to memories rooted in truth. Truth that for years had been blinded by misunderstandings and hate. She thought about all the things she'd loved about Sam—his honor, goodness, and integrity.

"I trust you." The sudden affirmation burst from her lips. She couldn't help it, even though she could tell he was still keeping something from her.

She was rewarded with Sam's wonderful smile. It was honest and real and it was a start.

Chapter 18

Sam was just finishing up a phone call when his lawyer arrived at his office. He lifted his hand and motioned for Chris to enter. When he finished the call he walked over to the credenza and poured himself a coffee.

"Thanks for coming, Chris. Coffee?"

"Yes, thanks."

Sam poured them both a cup while Chris pulled a sheaf of papers from his briefcase and slid a portion of them across the desk to Sam. Handing a steaming mug to Chris, Sam sat down and picked up one of the documents. For the next several minutes, they reviewed the provisions and terms of the partnership agreement between him and Kit, stopping several times when Sam had a question.

"As you can see, Kit still holds the majority of the estate, her two-thirds to your one-third. This, of course, will legitimize any updates your company may want to make to the property," Chris said.

That settled, Sam signed the document, laid the papers aside for Kit's signature, and moved on to the other issue concerning him. Anticipating Sam's request, Chris passed him the papers dealing with his father's will.

"Here's the will along with the codicil explaining the possessory interest your father set up for the Kendall family until your thirty-first birthday.

Sam leaned forward and picked up the copy of Adam Dawson's will, flipped to the add-on, and pulled it out. He read through it, nodded to Chris, and laid it aside to file later.

"And this," Chris slid another paper across the table, "is the document giving you clear title if you want it. You'd simply file it with our office and then it's done. Since your birthday is in a couple of weeks, I can handle that for you right now, if you'd like?"

Sam picked up the paper and tapped it with his fingers. "No. I want to put a stop to this. I have never wanted their home, nor do I want any more of their land. It's important to me they keep it."

Chris nodded. "Fine, we can handle that for you."

"I'm assuming I can ignore it, right?" Sam asked.

"You can, but I don't recommend it because if you die, the Kendalls will be notified their possessory interest is terminated and they will no longer be allowed to live there. But as the heir, you can quitclaim your interest in the property to them and essentially, it nullifies the codicil, once and for all. They never have to know it even existed."

"Then that's what I want to do. When can you get the quitclaim deed drawn up for me?"

"I can have it for you by tomorrow afternoon."

"I guess we're a go, then." He stood to his feet.

"Three at my office tomorrow?" Chris stood and gathered the materials.

Sam nodded. "I'll be there." The two slapped their hands together in a firm shake.

Sam saw Chris out, slipped on his jacket, then left the lodge.

In the parking lot, Sam double clicked on his key fob and slid behind the wheel of his truck. Just as he was about to pull onto the road, he realized he'd forgotten to put the documents away. He pulled to one side and slid his cell phone from his pocket. He punched in Diana's number, pressed send, then left her a message.

"Hey, Diana. There are some documents on my desk. File them when you get in, will you?"

He pressed end, then pulled out onto the road.

Relief, sure and solid, filled his soul. Finally, he could quit worrying, thankful Kit would always have the home she grew up in, and the business she'd worked so hard to build. The thought of her getting an eviction letter along with the added devastation that she didn't even own Sage Brush made him physically ill. Thank God that was behind him.

He drove over to see Kit, pretty darned pleased with himself. A weight had indeed lifted from his shoulders. He'd dodged a bullet for sure. In more ways than one.

It had been a week since Kit signed the partner agreement selling one-third of Sage Brush to Sam. After working out a schedule for the renovations, they made the joint decision to close the B&B so they could start immediately. After the financial stresses of the past year, Kit was thrilled to be managing the project. For the first time in months she was relaxed and confident. She was in her element and happier than she'd been in a long time. Living without the added worry of how she'd pay her bills was a blessing indeed.

She'd just hung up the phone with Randy of Gillian Electrical when the mail arrived. Shuffling through the contents, she tossed the junk, then placed the remaining mail on her desk.

"Hey, I just heard from Mom." Macy stuck her head in the doorway. "She said their flight out of Miami was cancelled due to bad weather and not to expect them for another two days."

"I wondered about that. I've been following that tropical storm on the news since yesterday. Let's hope it doesn't turn into a hurricane." Kit signed Trip's paycheck, then stuck it in an envelope. "Did she say where they were staying?"

"Yep. The Bayside Inn."

"That's fine." She wondered why her mom was emailing Macy instead of her.

"Oh, and she said not to worry, they'll be here for your birthday."

So that's why. "I told you, no party. Remember?"

Macy gave her big sister a bright smile causing Kit to roll her eyes.

"I mean it, kiddo. You know how I hate birthday parties." She closed the checkbook and slid it back in the cubby. "Are you on your way out?"

"Yeah. I'm going over to Becky's. We're going out for pizza and a movie. I might spend the night, since no one's here. Or, would you rather not be alone?"

"I won't be. Sam's coming over for dinner. I'm acting as contractor and he's going to help me set up the work schedule. But thanks for the offer. You go have fun."

"Okay, cool." Macy disappeared from the door.

Kit placed the rest of the checks in the designated envelopes and sealed them. She stood, stretched, then pulled together the material she'd need for her meeting with Sam.

The past week had been one of the happiest Sam had since returning to Sugar Creek. He'd almost forgotten what it was like not to focus every waking minute on a looming disaster. It was like watching a bomb squad slowly dismantle a ticking time bomb, not knowing whether they would be successful or not. Holding your breath at the snip of every wire. Experiencing a second of relief only to stress over the next step in the process, until realization comes that you can breathe a sigh knowing you've escaped the blast.

Last week, Chris ended up with an out-of-town emergency and had to stop by Sam's office on his way to the airport for his signature. When Sam signed the quitclaim he experienced the relief of escaping the blast. He'd never been more thankful of anything in his life. Chris assured him that signing was all Sam needed to do to nullify the codicil and that he'd file it as soon as he returned to town.

Satisfied, Sam had poured himself a glass of Macallan Scotch Single Malt 18 to celebrate. The board had been thrilled with his idea to merge with Kit's bed and breakfast and wondered why they hadn't thought of it sooner.

Truthfully, his heart was celebrating as he now drove over to Sage Brush, with a bottle of wine to toast their new partnership.

After removing the source of stress, he finally felt free to pursue her. The desire for a deeper relationship with Kit motivated and burned within him like a man in love. Because that's who he was. Stripped of all excuses, he was now free to court her. To love her.

This past week he could tell she'd warmed to him as well. He'd made an excuse to see her every day, just to see her light up when she answered the door or when he came upon her on horseback, or in town. Watching her heart open up to him was precious and her forgiving heart humbled him.

He pulled along the side of her house, parked his truck, and got out. Kit was holding open the kitchen door just as he stepped onto the back porch. She beamed up at him, making his heart pound with anticipation. One of the few times he'd kissed her was on the back steps of The Fat Canary. If one could call it that. It was much too sweet, over way too fast, and much too long ago. Hopefully, that would be rectified and soon.

"I hope I'm not too early."

"Not at all. I hope you're hungry. I made spaghetti and meat sauce." She chewed her lower lip, suddenly awkward.

She was adorable. Wearing a blue and white checked dress and sandals, she stood gazing up at him, her sparkling green eyes and copper bangs brushed appealingly across her delicate eyebrows. His racing heart drummed with anticipation.

"You look lovely. You make me wish I'd brought flowers."

"Oh." She made a face and waved her hand through the air. He'd embarrassed her. "But I see you brought wine." She quickly stepped aside for him to pass.

"That I did." He uncorked it while Kit grabbed two glasses from the cupboard. Once filled, they raised them in unison.

"To our first week as partners," Kit said.

"And here's to many more." The chink of crystal sealed the deal, then he followed Kit to the stove. "Is that apple pie I smell?"

"No, I'm just drying apples for the horses. They smell great don't they?"

"I'll say." He drew in a deep breath. "So, you're still making them, huh?"

"Sure am." She glanced up at him, her eyes filled with mirth. "Remember the day we went to Miller's grocery to buy apples for my mom, so Maggie could make pies for our guests, and Mr. Miller gave us that huge box of overripe apples for the horses?"

"I do." Sam chuckled, knowing what was coming.

"We'd cut them all up. Took us hours and then we left to do something, I can't remember now. But when we got back Maggie had thrown them all away."

"And was madder than a wet hen, thinking we'd bought rotten apples for her guests." He laughed. "And then you started to cry because we'd done all that work."

"And then you commenced to tell her that *her* apples were in the fridge."

He watched Kit bubble up with laugher. Sparkling beautiful laughter. He smiled down at her, drinking in every single moment.

"As I recall, she did make up for it by helping us dig our apples out of the trash."

"She sure did." Kit gazed up at him, all glowing and sparkly eyed. She bit her lower lip and turned back to the tomato sauce simmering on the stove.

"Here, stir while I get the pasta going." Kit handed him a large wooden spoon, before turning on another burner to boil water for the pasta.

"This sauce smells great. I didn't know you could cook."

"You'd be surprised what I've learned since you went away."

Something about the way she said it bothered him for a second. But when he saw her smile, he relaxed.

"And stop your flattering, Sam. I'll be thinking you want something." She playfully cocked her head to the side as she reached for the box of pasta.

"I do want something." He rested the spoon against the pot and turned her toward him. "I've missed you, Kit."

Kit froze along with the pasta box and stared at him. Her lovely cheeks turned the color of fresh, summer peaches and her wide eyes held the barest hint of anxiety.

"You have?" She licked her lips at least a half dozen times and stood silent and waiting.

He nodded never taking his eyes off her sweet pixie face. Adoration and expectation flowed from her green eyes.

Yup. She loves me all right.

Then, as if released from a spell, she suddenly realized what she was doing. She hastily removed the fork from the boiling water, then quickly dumped in the pasta, pressing her hand over the mass of spikes until all was submerged.

Elated at her reaction, he'd forgotten to watch his own simmering pot. After a quick stir, he lifted the sauce spoon to her mouth. "Here, taste," he said.

When the thick red tomato sauce mingled with her pink lipstick, something in his gut flipped and churned, and made him hungry for more than spaghetti.

"Mmm, that is good." She pressed her lips together in satisfaction, then smiled up at him.

God her eyes were beautiful. She was beautiful.

"Here, I'll take that." Kit plucked the spoon from his hand. "Why don't you finish setting the table?"

Just as he stepped away, Kit yelped and jumped back. The sauce had bubbled up, spitting red in all directions.

Kit quickly lowered the eye to a simmer, stepped over to the sink, and turned on the faucet.

"Are you okay?" he asked as she stuck her arm under the cold running water.

"Yeah, it'll be fine. It just stings a little." After several seconds, she shut off the valve and reached for a paper towel.

Sam lifted an apron off a nearby hook, then looped the top part over Kit's head. When he slid his arms around her waist to tie it in the back, he left them there. Gently and ever so slowly, he pulled her into his arms.

He was done waiting.

Her glistening eyes and soft parted lips were all the invitation he needed. Lowering his head, he placed his lips on hers. Warm and supple, they tasted of sweet peppers and oregano. He lifted his lips from hers and reveled in her soft moan as he nuzzled the soft spot behind her ear. Citrus and vanilla engulfed his senses as he explored the nape of her neck.

"Oh, Sam." Kit sighed and clung to him.

His breath quickened and he groaned. The way she said his name. It tumbled from her lips like cool water on a blistering hot day, satisfying his thirst and his soul. He was transported back to the night when she'd told him she loved him. He longed to hear those words again, but timing was everything. He knew he'd hear them when she fully trusted him again. No matter how long it took, he would regain her trust.

His lips found hers again, this time crushing in his hunger to possess her, starving for her affection and her love.

Kit pulled away and gazed up at him. "Sammy, are you sure?"

"I've never been more certain of anything in my life," he said, in a husky voice, then kissed her again like his life depended on it.

Her arms tighten around his neck, and her slender body pressed against his, sending his quickening pulse into overtime.

Just as he started to lose himself in her embrace, a stomping sound echoed from the back porch. Sam lifted his head and Kit's eyes flew open. Each questioning the other as to what that could be.

"Did you hear that?" he asked.

"Footsteps."

"Yes."

Macy burst through the kitchen door right as they separated.

Sam gripped the spoon handle and held his breath, outwardly calm as he stirred the tomato sauce with Kit looking over his shoulder as if she were checking its progress. He hoped like the devil they didn't look guilty. How he parted from her that fast amazed even him. He felt like a teenager who'd just been caught making out by his mother. Not the best of feelings. He glanced over at Kit and almost doubled over at the mirth in her eyes. He exhaled in relief. Kit was completely under control, like she'd had previous experience with this sort of thing.

"Hi, kiddo. I thought you were out for the evening?" Kit asked calmly.

Macy plopped down and propped her elbow on the back of the chair. "Naw, it didn't work out. Becky had to go see her grandparents this evening so I'm going over tomorrow, instead." She heaved a sigh. "So. What's for dinner?"

Sam glanced at Kit, pleased to see her eyes held a twinkle and the promise of later.

Chapter 19

The next afternoon, Kit entered her office just as Macy came downstairs. She was her usual cute self, dressed in a sleeveless top and shorts. She ducked in the office with her floral backpack slung over her shoulder, stuffed to the max with overnight gear.

"Looks like you're staying for a week. You *are* planning to come back sometime, aren't you?" Kit teased.

"I don't know? I'd sure hate to interrupt you and Sam again," Macy replied with a twinkle. "Maybe you should tell me when I *can* come home."

Kit gave Macy her sweetest smile. "Trust me, you're not interrupting anything there."

"That's not what it looked like to me."

"Get outta here."

Macy giggled, gave Kit a hug then left.

Kit was still smiling when she turned back to her paper-laden desk. For the first time in months the stack of mail staring up at her didn't make her stomach churn. With her bills finally paid off, she no longer had to worry about past due notices and collection agencies. The property taxes would also be paid on time, thanks to Sam's investment.

She scooted up to the desk, then shuffled deftly through the stack like a dealer in a poker game. Her hand stilled.

What's this?

Something from Baker, Billings & Blackwell PLLC, the same law firm that had represented Adam Dawson against her father. She ripped it open, her forehead creased as she scanned the contents.

A sudden lurch followed by a sinking feeling slammed into her stomach. Her hands shook as she reread the letter. Her mind reeled. She jumped to her feet. Pacing the floor like a caged lion, her breaths came in short, staccato gasps. Then suddenly, she couldn't breath and clutched the letter to her chest.

She couldn't have been more hurt than if Sam had punched her in the face. Tears stung the back of her eyelids but she refused to cry. Numb, she tried to pull herself together. There had to be an explanation. This could not be happening.

Kit walked slowly toward the massive front entrance of McCabe's Resort Lodge, completely ignoring the bellman's smile and friendly greeting. She passed through the large foyer unaware of the sweet and savory smells coming from the hot tea and scones being served in the area.

She made her way to the suite of offices, unaware of Sharon and Diana and all the others milling around their desks and comfortable chairs.

"May I help you?" Sharon asked, looking uncomfortable when she received no answer.

"Ma'am, are you all right," another office worker asked.

Kit ignored all of them. Determined and heartsick, all she could think about was putting one foot in front of the other as she neared Sam's private office.

"You can't go in there. He's in a meeting." Diana said.

Kit continued on, disregarding every comment, muting every sound. Facing Sam's office door, she turned the handle and entered.

Startled, Sam snapped his head in her direction.

Kit held the letter out to him. "What is this?"

Sam held his breath, then stood slowly. Something was terribly wrong. "Excuse me for a moment, will you?" He looked pointedly at the two gentlemen. "I think this is a good time for refreshments. Diana will take care of you." Sam pasted on a smile as he watched the two men walk out. "Sam. I'm sorry. I tried to stop her." Diana insisted, obviously infuriated, but at Sam's nod she left, closing the door behind her.

Kit's dark, accusatory eyes stared up at him. Her face cold and pale. A marble statue had more life than she did at that moment. He took a tentative step toward her and pulled the letter from her fingers.

"Is it true?"

As soon as he saw the document, he blanched. This was not possible.

"Where did you get this?"

"It says I don't own Sage Brush and haven't for the past six years." A gut-wrenching sound tumbled from her lips, the words cutting his heart like a razor. "It says on August 10th, on your birthday, I have to relinquish the property." Desperate, questioning eyes pleaded with him for it not to be true.

Defeat, measured and full, punched him in his ribs. He wanted to crush the damn thing. Destroy it. But crushed or not it was still there in black and white. Filed and sent out. How the hell did this happen? No one had authority to file, much less send this letter.

"Kit, listen to me."

"Just answer the question." She stood in front of him, frightened and tense. Her eyes filled with dread as she waited for his answer, her ashen complexion delivering guilt by the truckload.

He heaved a sigh. "Part of it's true. Yes. But, I didn't okay this." He jabbed his finger at the letter. "I don't know how this happened, but believe me, I intend to find out."

She shook her head. "No more explanations." She stood perfectly still and her eyes darkened with sadness.

There was so much that needed to be said but Sam knew it would be impossible for him to try and explain it all in that moment.

He grabbed hold of her arms. "Kit, honey. I know this is a shock, but I want you to sit tight until I find out what happened. Promise me."

Kit didn't say a word. She shrugged out of his grasp and stared at him. He watched her eyes fill with distrust and loathing, before she slowly turned and walked out the door. He didn't move, just watched her go. Knowing it was too late for words.

After Kit left, he looked closely at the document in his hands. He didn't sign this. Anger flared in his gut. There was only one person who had access to this file.

Sam stepped into the outer offices. Sharon was walking down the corridor with his two guests. Good, they were still occupied.

He made his way to Diana's office and opened the door. Diana's eyes lit up at his appearance, then just as quickly shuddered in apprehension.

"This time you went too far," he stated grimly, slapping the letter down on her desk. It took every ounce of self-control not to drag her from her chair and throw her out. "I swear, if you were a man . . ."

Diana's perfectly powdered face turned white. Her self-assured poise crumbled. "I thought you wanted me to file it. Your voice mail clearly said—"

He shook his head. "Sorry, naïve doesn't suit you. When I said file it, I meant in a drawer. And that's not my signature." He slapped the paper with his hand. "It won't hold up. You knew that and sent it anyway." He sucked in a sharp breath. "I warned you, Diana. Not this town and not my friends. Now get out."

Diana shot to her feet. "That girl has caused you nothing

but trouble." She spread her hands out toward him. "I did it for you, for *us*."

"There is no *us*. Now, pack your things and go." He turned on his heels and left.

Kit stood in her kitchen, suddenly and completely overwhelmed. She felt numb, dead really. She'd worked for a long time to make the B&B a success but now it was over. It wasn't even hers anymore. Her brain turned to mush as she tried to make sense of it.

She stood in the middle of the kitchen, at a total loss. What should she do? Pack? But what? One moment her mind was numb; the next it seemed to race around in panic. She stood motionless, trying to think, then walked to the storage room to grab several small boxes.

A moment later she was at her desk. She slowly picked up a file, looked at it, then set it back down. A cloud of darkness overcame her. A wave of nausea engulfed her forcing her to close her eyes, she grabbed the edge of the desk for support. She took slow, deep breaths until she could see clearly. She opened a drawer, then closed it. She had no idea what to do. Stepping to the bookcase, she began pulling her books off the shelves.

Sam slammed on the breaks of his black Ford truck and came to a screeching halt. He noticed Kit's Chevy was parked at the side of the house. Except for that, Sage Brush looked deserted. He jumped out as soon as he cut the engine and bounded up the front steps.

He tried the door handle but it was locked. "Kit! Open up!" When pounding on the door produced no answer, he ran around back and let himself in through the kitchen.

The under-counter lights were on, but the rooms beyond were in darkness. He walked through the kitchen to the front hall and called out for her, but got no response. When he entered the living room he switched on a lamp, turned and saw her standing in the office in the semi-darkness.

"Kit." He spoke softly so not to startle her.

She turned toward him. Even though her eyes were hollow, poise and dignity were in her bearing. She stood before him as if she were on the way to the guillotine. God he loved her. Even when she thought she'd lost it all, she was so brave. His eyes darted to the stacks of books and open file drawers.

"Have you come so soon? I thought I'd at least have a few days."

"Kit, for God's sake—"

"To get organized," she said. "I hope that's okay."

She spread her hands and looked around the office. "There's so much to sort out. I know it must look like a mess, but—"

"Please. Come sit with me and let me tell you what happened."

She continued to ramble, her words tumbling from her lips like a babbling brook. In two strides, Sam took her by the shoulders and gently turned her toward him.

"Look at me, honey."

She stopped talking and gazed up at him. Defeat poured from her clouded, sorrowful eyes. He'd seen a lot of emotions on Kit's face, but never that. A brave, last stand that kicked him in the ribs. She was devastated. She'd given up. And in that moment self-loathing gripped him by the collar and shook him senseless. He'd never meant for her to find out. All he ever wanted to do was to protect her. God he just wanted to hold her, to kiss her. But knew she'd have none of him.

She didn't say a word. Just raised her arms and pushed out of his grasp.

He dropped his hands to his sides and watched her turn from him to continue her packing. If you could call it that. She kept making little piles and stacks around the room. She seemed disoriented. He'd heard of such things happening to people after a traumatic event. They'd walk around, sometimes for hours, engaged in mundane tasks, completely unaware of what they were doing. Anxiety tore through him like a paper shredder.

He couldn't take it anymore. He scooped her in his arms.

"No!" Kit screamed, then pummeled his chest with her fists. When that proved impotent, she pushed and plied her fingers against his arms until he bled.

He clenched his teeth against the pain, then carried her, kicking and yelling, up the stairs to her bedroom.

"You can come at me with all you've got. But, you're going to hear me out."

When he set her down she bolted for the door. He quickly encircled his arm around her waist and pinned her to his side. Somehow he managed to turn the key with his free hand locking them both in. He slipped the key into his jeans, then released her. She came at him all fists, landing a jab smack against his jaw. Kit then raised her leg in a high kick that would have had him singing soprano if he hadn't jumped to the side at the last second. He swore, grabbed hold of her waist, spun her around, and pinned her against his chest.

"Let go of me!"

He didn't answer, just let her rail at him until she was sobbing and exhausted, lying limp in his arms.

His breaths came in huge gulps but he wasn't about to release her until he was sure he was safe. A wildcat would've been less trouble.

When he felt it was safe to let her go he slowly lessened his hold, led her to the bed, then pulled her in his arms.

Minutes later, she pushed out of his embrace, then

curled up on her bed with her back to him. "Please go," she whispered.

Sam stood to his feet and looked down at her. Curled up in a knot, her hair a tangled mess, she looked like a waif. And as for her hearing him out, well, that was no longer an option. She'd shut him out, and it hurt like hell.

He ran his hand around the back of his neck, a sorry remedy for the knot of tension that had settled there. He sighed heavily and left the room.

When Kit woke up, it was late morning. She stared at the ceiling, then felt a wave of sickness slam into her midsection as she recalled the previous night's events. She sat up, threw off the covers, then glanced around the room. Funny how one event could make everything look different from one day to the next. She opened her closet and pulled out her suitcase, then realized she had nowhere to go. Besides, her mother was coming back tomorrow. Her mind was in a complete muddle. She needed caffeine. When she entered the kitchen Sam was sitting at the table with a cup of coffee. She hesitated in the doorway when she saw him.

"I made coffee." He stood and poured her a mug.

She licked her lips and walked over to the table. "Thanks." She slid into the seat across from him, took a sip, then looked up to find his eyes on her.

"Sam, last night . . ." She slid her finger around the lip of the mug.

"It's all right, honey."

Kit lowered her eyes to her cup. "It's not. I've never lost it like that."

He reached across the table and took her hand in his. "You were in shock, plus you've been under a lot of stress. It's perfectly understandable."

She noticed the scratches on his arms and drew in a sharp breath. "Did I do that?" She reached out and gently ran her fingers over the raw areas.

"You were quite the little wildcat. Truthfully, I feared for my manhood at one point." He chuckled.

"It's not funny." She snatched her hand from his arm and jumped to her feet.

"Okay, fine. No more joking. Please sit and listen to what I have to say."

Kit sighed and sat back down.

"First of all, as far as I'm concerned, this is your home."

"Oh, please."

"I mean it. What would I do with this place? I can only think of one use for it, and that I plan on keeping to myself for the time being."

Her eyes darted to his. Good. He'd gotten her attention. He knew her. Knew she liked nothing better than a bit of mystery and was relieved to see a glimmer of hope back in her eyes.

"Second, that document no longer applies. It's not even legal. I met with my lawyer over a week ago to discuss several things concerning my father's estate and this was one of them. He'd drawn up the papers thinking I was going to file. But I told him not to. Instead, I sent him back to draw up the quitclaim signifying I was giving up my rights to the property. I signed them the next day."

"Then how did this happen?"

"I left Diana a note to file the papers on my desk. Instead, she read it, signed it, then sent it to my law firm."

"Why would she do that?"

"She's a vindictive woman. Maybe she was jealous of our relationship. I don't know. But she's gone. I fired her. What she did was cruel and malicious and I'm deeply sorry. You were never to know."

"Never to know? I'm not a child, Sam. This, I needed to know. And before now."

"I know. I realize that now. But, no matter what happened between our fathers, I'd never take your home from you."

"But you did, Sam. I have the document to prove it."

Chapter 20

"Hello, we're home. Kit? Macy?" Daisy called out while she held the door for her husband who followed behind carrying two large suitcases.

Macy yelped, ran downstairs, and flung herself into her mother's arms.

Daisy laughed and hugged Macy like she hadn't seen her youngest daughter in years instead of months. Releasing her mom, Macy then flung herself at Jeff, who swung her around before putting her down.

Kit was right behind, having put on her 'happy' face so as not to worry her mom. Even though her heart was broken, she shared laughter and hugs with the honeymooners.

Maggie joined them just as suitcases were opened and gifts were given.

"Kit, don't open those now. They're for your birthday," Daisy said.

"Today *is* my birthday," Kit teased her mom.

"You know what I mean." Then gave Kit a playful slap on her hand as she pretended to pull on the brightly colored ribbon.

"Okay, y'all. Lunch is ready," Maggie called everybody to the kitchen where she'd set the table for Daisy and Jeff's homecoming feast. The spread consisted of all Daisy's favorites, fried chicken, creamed potatoes, field peas, and hot biscuits sharing the lineup.

Piling in around the large pine farm table, they sat down and held hands for the blessing. Jeff led a sweet prayer of thanksgiving for their safe arrival and Maggie's wonderful home-cooked meal.

When lunch was over and everyone had had their fill, Maggie shooed everyone out of the kitchen while she cleaned up.

"I don't know about you ladies, but after being cooped up in a hotel for thirty-six hours then another five in the Miami airport, I am ready for some sunshine." Jeff winked at Macy. "How about a ride, Missy."

"Race you to the barn." Macy bolted out the back door.

"You're on, young lady." Jeff yelled after her.

Daisy and Kit followed them out and headed for the creek.

"This is so nice," Daisy said. "I've always loved taking walks along here. August is way too hot for horseback riding. I don't know how those two stand it."

"It's funny how much alike they are, isn't it? Not being related and all." Kit watched the two of them lead their mounts from the barn.

"I know. I'm glad Macy has someone like Jeff while she's still growing up."

"Me, too." Kit smiled at her mother.

Daisy placed an arm over Kit's shoulder and gave her a quick hug. "The place looks wonderful, honey. The Kendall stamp is all over it. Your daddy would have been so proud of you."

"Thanks, Mom."

As they strolled along, Kit glanced at her mother's serene face wondering if she should dare broach the subject that burned in her chest.

"What is it, sweetie?"

Kit's steps faltered, then she shot a quick glance at the ground. "What do you mean?"

"Oh, I don't know. All through lunch you just seemed preoccupied."

Kit stopped by one of the oaks that lined the creek, plucked a stray Blue Bonnet from the ground, and twirled it between her fingers. "First Maggie and now you. Am I that transparent?"

Daisy smoothed Kit's bangs away from her forehead. "You have the most expressive eyes. You inherited that from your father. He was also very easy to read."

Kit thought about the night her father ran from Mr. Dawson's office and suddenly she ached for him, fully understanding his pain. Kit scuffed at a pebble with the toe of her boot. "Mom, this is going to seem a bit out of left field, but I've been wondering about it for a long time. How exactly did Dad lose our property?"

Daisy's eyes grew serious. "Let's keep walking." She linked her arm through Kit's. "Your father was a gambler. Plain and simple. A deck of cards was his Achilles' heel. If there was a poker game around, he'd find it. Even if it was in the next county."

"So he lost it in a card game?"

"I'm afraid so." Daisy shrugged. "Not long after that, he started losing interest in running the ranch."

"I remember."

Daisy nodded. "Instead of accepting what he'd done and moving on, he started drinking more and more. He became broody and argumentative and hell-bent on getting his property back. As a result, he tried one hair-brained scheme after another until he finally lost everything—his dignity, his inner drive, and his self-esteem."

"But he never lost you, did he? You were always there for him."

Daisy stopped and gazed out over the land. "He was my knight till the end. Unfortunately, he lost the shine from his armor."

"I'm sorry, Mom." Kit stared at the ground, angry with herself for bringing it up. But she was into it now. She needed to keep going.

"Mom. I don't know how to tell you this except to just come out and say it. When you said Dad lost everything, well he did. Literally. Dad lost the bed and breakfast. We don't own it anymore. We haven't for years."

"What?" Startled, Daisy turned toward Kit, utterly dumbfounded.

Suddenly, everything just spilled out. Kit told Daisy about Adam Dawson's will and filled her in on the details of the codicil.

Daisy shook her head. "Then that explains why Don quit working the ranch. He loved the land so much. I knew the only reason he'd ever quit working it would've been because he'd lost it. I suspected as much at the time and fully expected us to be evicted, but when nothing happened I assumed I'd been wrong."

"And he never said anything about it?"

"No. Nothing."

Kit then told her the lengths Sam had gone through to protect her from ever finding out about it, even going so far as to offer to buy them out two years ago."

"That was Sam?"

"Yes." She finished by sharing Diana's diabolical part in the whole thing and Sam's insistence that Sage Brush was still hers.

"Well that doesn't surprise me one bit. Even though he was young, Sam was a tremendous help to me during those years with your father. He stepped in the gap, as if he were your father's son."

Kit's eyes flew to her mother's face. "What do you mean?"

"Sam took over where your father left off and if not for him we'd have lost Sage Brush to the bank long before we ever lost it to Adam Dawson. The three years Sam was foreman we actually made a profit." Daisy let out a long heartfelt sigh. "I can't even tell you how many nights he brought your father home after he'd been drinking. Helping me put him to bed." She shook her head. "It was a difficult time."

Kit gnawed at her lower lip. "Mom, I'm so confused. The Dawsons were always takers. First our land, then our oil. I want to trust Sam, but after everything that's happened. I just don't know if I can."

"I understand your frustration. And I'm not making any excuses for Adam but he did offer your father half of the profits. In some ways he was a decent man. Forgiveness is hard to give. But once you do, the blessing flows to your side."

Kit realized she'd seen her father through the eyes of an adoring daughter. To be hit with the truth about his weaknesses was hard to bear, but if she were completely honest, she'd have to admit she'd known it all along. Heck, hadn't she spent the last six years trying to take his place? Trying to be what he wasn't?

Kit felt like crying. "How could I have missed so much?"

"You were a teenager. Out with your friends."

"Off playing when I should have been paying more attention."

"Don't be so hard on yourself. You were your daddy's little girl."

"Spoiled, you mean."

"Not at all. You adored your father and there's nothing wrong with that. He knew how much you loved this land. I'm sure that's why he kept all of this from us, from you."

"It's amazing how a good dose of reality can awaken a person. Losing our land devastated me. Nothing was the same after that."

Daisy gently touched Kit's cheek. "Your father made a lot of choices in his life, some good and some not so good. He gambled and lost and you have to accept that."

"That doesn't negate the fact Adam Dawson took advantage of him."

"That may well be. But you can't blame the son for the father's sins. Anymore than someone should blame you for your father's." Daisy placed her hands on Kit's shoulders and looked her square in the face. "You're strong, Kit. You'll get through this. We'll get through this."

Kit nodded and glanced back at the house. "At least Macy and I got to grow up here. But I should've let you sell it when you had the chance."

"What? And miss the courageous, self-assured young woman you've become? Not a chance."

Even though she felt rotten, Kit couldn't help but smile. Her mother always knew how to get her daughters to brighten up.

"And I'm glad to see you're finally letting your hair grow out."

Kit rolled her eyes and laughed.

"There, that's better," Daisy gave Kit a smile of her own. "You know, sweetie, I've been blessed to experience love twice now in my life. So, I recognize it when I see it. You know what I think?"

Kit shook her head.

"I think any man who goes to those lengths is a man in love. Now, go take another walk while I help your sister with your birthday party."

As she watched her mom walk away, Kit thought of the sermon she'd heard all those weeks ago. There were all kinds of giants one had to conquer. And right now she stood face-to-face with one of her own making. Bitterness and anger had driven her far too long. It was time to cast the stone and kill her giant. In that moment she forgave Adam Dawson, she forgave her father, and she forgave herself.

As Kit sauntered along the creek she mulled over the things her mom had told her about Sam. It seemed she, too, thought he was near perfect. She heard a distant rumble and looked up. A few dark clouds had formed overhead cooling down the area and bringing a refreshing breeze to her sweaty upper lip and brow. As she continued to stroll, she wondered how long she needed to give them inside the house. She smiled to herself. She'd come upon Maggie and Macy several times, whispering with their heads together only to see them snap apart like they were planning a bank robbery or something. Macy was so transparent, thinking she could put anything over on her.

Her thoughts turned to Sam. Today was his birthday, too. Should she go over to the lodge and wish him a happy birthday? No matter what happened, she knew he'd give her plenty of time to move out. Months, more than likely. It pained her to think about it, but honestly, he'd had no control over what his father had done. Heck, even he didn't like his father. She took a deep breath. Yes, she'd bring him a gift. Just a little something. A token of sorts, bringing healing to their relationship. But, did they even have a relationship? She scuffed her boot against the dry earth. Had she totally blown it with him?

A sudden flash of rope skimmed across Kit's vision, stopping her in her tracks. She inhaled sharply, then squealed as the lasso jerked tightly around her torso pinning her arms to her sides. Knowing full well who'd be at the other end, she craned her neck over her shoulder, anyway.

With a deft maneuver, Sam gave a small jerk spinning her around to face him. Digging her heels in the dirt proved no help at all as he pulled her closer and closer. His dress shirt was rolled up at the sleeves revealing strong forearms that rippled with each movement. Hand over hand, he pulled her toward him.

Kit clenched her teeth, all thoughts of healing their relationship gone. It was maddening to be this weak. She yanked against the lasso, twisting and turning to get free. She so wished she were a man.

Sam gently tugged on the rope until she was standing right in front of him.

Her chest heaved. "What do you think—?"

Sam pulled her to him and planted a kiss against her lips. He lifted his head, then gave her a look that made her go weak at the knees. That glimmer of amusement in his eyes wasn't lost on her either. In fact, it made her fighting mad. She licked her lips. "I mean it, Sam. Let me—"

Sam laid another kiss on her. This time his firm lips covered hers with such force her knees buckled. He lifted his head and caught her against his chest just as the rope loosened.

"Go." She finished. Heady from his nearness and his aftershave, Kit had to take a moment to steady her weak limbs.

"Are we finished? May I speak now?" he asked.

Kit raised her chin and eyed him with a promise that she wasn't even close to finished.

"Yesterday, you needed proof. Well, today I have it." He removed a letter from his back pocket, unfolded it with the snap of his hand, then planted it right in front of her face.

Kit had no choice but to read the document. It was the quitclaim.

"So?"

He heaved a sigh, then shook his head. "Look at the date."

It was clearly dated before the other one, proving it had been filed first. Her chin lowered, the haughty tilt disappearing as she realized what Sam had done for her. She thought of what her mother had said earlier. *Any man who goes to those lengths is a man in love.* Maybe she should put that to the test. She gazed into his beautiful eyes. The eyes are the windows to the soul, right? Then surely, if he loved her . . .

"I don't accept charity," she blurted out.

"It's a birthday gift."

Disappointment washed over her. She dropped her eyes and stared at a button on his shirt. "Sorry, I can't accept. That's way too expensive. Plus, as a Kendall, I insist on paying my debts."

Sam lifted her chin with his hand. "You're right. That's way too expensive for a mere birthday." His aquamarine eyes darkened with desire. "Then think of it as a wedding present. And as for the debts, well, I can think of several ways I could collect on our honeymoon."

Kit's heart thumped and clattered noisily within her chest. *Did he just propose?* Open-mouthed, she stared up at him.

"Any questions?" he asked with the confidence of a man who already knew the answers.

With her last ounce of bravado, she tried to fold her arms across her chest but couldn't because of the lasso. "Are you bribing me?"

"If that's what it takes." He shrugged. Then his lips parted in that old familiar smile and she was undone. Totally and completely. She was fully aware she stood looking at him like some adoring puppy, but no matter. She loved this man and if she'd read his cards right, he loved her, too.

"Actually, I do have one more question."

"Well?" he asked, when she hesitated.

"When are you going to untie me so I can kiss you back?"

"I don't know?" A cagey grin appeared on his handsome face. "I kind of like you here. Makes me feel all masculine and in control."

"Trust me. It's an illusion. But, I'm more than happy for you to go on thinking it."

"Okay, but on one condition." He cocked his head to one side with a smile in his eyes.

"Which is?"

"Tell me you love me."

Kit ran her tongue over dry lips. "I love you, Sammy."

He smiled, his blue eyes softening as he scanned her face. "And, I love you."

She caught her breath at the sweet hunger in their depths.

Sam pulled her, lasso and all, into his arms and as he started to lift the rope from around her, he stopped. "Uh, there's just one more thing." He eyed her with a look somewhere between amusement and contrition.

"Now what?" It was all she could do not to stomp her feet.

"I own The Fat Canary. And, you're fired."

Her mouth fell open like a flytrap. "Well, I'll be a—"

Sam's lips covered hers in another quick mouth-shutting kiss.

"You know, if you're gonna do that every time I try to say something, then we're going to have a heck of a time making conversation."

"There's all kinds of communication, sweetheart and I'm partial to this kind." He entwined his fingers in her copper strands and kissed her again.

A heart-stopping, mind-whirling, kiss.

He was killing her. She knew it and he did, too. When he raised his head, she lifted her chin and gave him her best, 'I could care less' look.

"Is that it? Anything else I should know before you release me?" she asked, hoping he'd think he hadn't phased her one little bit. But she knew by the expression on his face that she'd failed miserably.

"Only that I love you." And as he loosened the rope at Kit's waist, he gave her a look that said he knew perfectly well what his kisses did to her. Sam gathered her close, just as the lasso hit the dirt. "Honey, you've been pulling my strings for years. You just haven't realized it."

Kit gazed into Sam's gorgeous eyes before closing hers to receive his kiss. She melted into his embrace and for the first time in years, she experienced joy as Sam wrapped her in his arms, his kiss deepening, forever dispelling any doubts that he loved her.

Sam lifted his head to nuzzle her ear. "When we're married you can expect something along these lines at least twice a day," he said as he continued to explore the soft nape of her neck.

"Only twice?" she replied, breathless and near giddy.

Sam groaned and put her away from him. "Come on. They're waiting for us inside."

"What? Oh, yeah. Macy's been planning this for weeks. We'd better go."

They hadn't taken two steps before Sam swung her back in his arms. Kissing her as if he knew it would be hours before he could do it again. Urgency exploded within him and she responded to his kiss with a need of her own. Her mind reeled as his aftershave released a flood of memories. Good memories, reminding her of all they'd had and would continue to have in the days to come. It was like a rainfall, spilling over and around her.

Suddenly, a drop of water hit her face, then another. They pulled apart, blinking against the wet as they looked to the heavens. Rain. Cool. Refreshing and one hundred percent pure. Kit briefly closed her eyes, then lifted her hands and face to the cascading drops. Sam laughed, grabbed her around the waist and swung her through the air. He stole a quick kiss, then took hold of her hand and together they ran back to the house.

They burst through the back door and laughingly shook off the wet.

"Happy Birthday!"

Shouts came from all across the room.

Kit spun and her jaw dropped. The kitchen was packed with all the people she cared about. While Maggie ordered her husband to get more chairs, Trip stood patiently waiting for cake with his arm around Tess. Elena was seated and looked ready to pop and Jake and their boys smiled at her from across the room, the youngest one hanging on Jake's pant leg. Daisy and Jeff stood off to the side wreathed in smiles. Streamers were hanging from the ceiling and brightly wrapped presents were stacked at one end of the pine table. The smell of freshly brewed coffee and sweet cake filled the air.

Macy skipped over and hugged her. "Are you surprised?"

She playfully gave Macy the evil eye. "I'll deal with you later."

Everyone burst out laughing.

"Come look at your gorgeous cake," Macy bubbled. "Maggie outdid herself as usual."

Sam slid his fingers through his damp hair then placed his hand against Kit's back as they followed Macy to the far side of the table. A large three-tiered cake slathered with thick, butter cream icing sat at the far end. The cake was adorned with stacks upon stacks of sweet yellow roses, which until this moment had hidden the inscription from Kit's view.

Happy Birthday Kit and Sam was beautifully painted in blue icing across the top.

Kit caught her breath, then glanced at Maggie, who gave her that 'I knew all along' look.

Kit turned to Sam and watched his eyes light up as he read the words on the cake. Their cake.

"I see your name is now first."

She loved the way his eyes crinkled at the corners when he smiled at her. That roguish tilt of his lips all but melting her bones.

"As it should be," she teased back.

When Macy lit the candles a hushed silence fell over the room.

"Make a wish!" the children shouted, their words falling from their little mouths like dominoes.

"Together?" Sam asked.

At Kit's nod, they leaned forward at their waists and inhaled. When they blew out the candles, applause and cheers went up around the large kitchen.

"Okay, time to cut the cake," Trip announced. "Here, give me that knife," he added, when Maggie proved to be too slow. On Trip's nod, Jake grabbed the vanilla ice cream from the freezer and started scooping. The children gathered around the table, wide-eyed, in anticipation of the marvelous confection standing before them.

Sam took that moment to pull Kit aside. The chink of china and coffee cups faded to the background as Kit gazed up into his eyes. The startling blue depths were filled with love as he looked down at her. Oblivious to the noises and activity around her, Kit wrapped her arms around Sam's neck and pulled him to her. Even though her kiss was sweet and tender, it held a promise of more to come.

"We don't want to shock the kids," she teased.

"No, we don't." He chuckled.

"Happy Birthday, Sammy."

"And to you, sweetheart."

CPSIA information can be obtained at www.ICGtesting.com
Printed in the USA
LVOW01s0510230714

395537LV00008B/18/P